I0745440

USA TODAY BESTSELLING AUTHOR

ALLYSON LINDT

This book is a work of fiction.

While reference might be made to actual historical events or existing locations, the names, characters, places, and incidents are either the product of the author's imagination or are used fictitiously, and any resemblance to actual persons, living or dead, business establishments, events, or locales is entirely coincidental.

*To every geek girl,
everywhere,
trust yourself.*

Chapter One

The one thing that made crunch time tolerable was my boss. It wasn't his fault we were working eighty-hour weeks to wrap up our company's most anticipated game ever; he took his directions from the people above him, like the rest of us.

Besides, even at eleven at night, when had both been staring at the same code problem for the last three hours and were punchy from lack of sleep, he was gorgeous. Dark hair that was cut close, piercing dark eyes, and tonight, a tantalizing hint of stubble.

Luke clucked. "Anne, Anne, Anne… Why the fuck isn't this working, Anne?"

"Gremlins?" I loved the way my name rolled off his tongue. And I was too tired to pretend I didn't want other bits of me on his tongue as well. I also didn't have any better answer to his question than any other time he'd asked it tonight.

We were in his office. As a director, he got one of the mid-range offices, with room for a small table in the corner and a great view of the mountains. I was sit-leaning against the edge of his polished-wood desk, watching him work. God, I loved the view. It almost made up for the fact that we were working on a Sunday.

Luke had returned to the flow chart we started an hour ago, and was drawing another series of lines. He jabbed the marker into the board several times, leaving a series of ink freckles. "The hobbits had a more direct, easy route walking to Mordor. Who wrote this shit?"

It didn't matter that his question wasn't funny. I still had to cut off my laugh before it became one of those drawn-out, sleep-deprived giggles. "We did."

I'd had more coffee in the last week than I used to drink in a year. Anything with high amounts of caffeine had been added to my *Best Friends* list since this project went sideways, shit itself, and landed face down, ass up in a ditch at the bottom of a deep ravine. Laughing was one of the only ways to stay sane in the midst of it all.

He sighed and dropped the marker. It clattered against the tray and bounced to the ground. "In hindsight, we should have just chartered a helicopter and flown into the mountain. The direct path is always the best."

And it was rarely the path a group of developers took. Partly because we all had different

waiting for it

definitions of *direct.* "I'm at the point where I'd sell my soul to Sauron to fix this issue. I wouldn't hesitate."

"You'd make a horrible ring wraith. The hood and eternal damnation would obscure those gorgeous eyes." He turned back to the board and bent at the waist to pick up the marker, the muscles along his back and arms rippling under his T-shirt. He was a Marine-turned-developer and still had the physique.

"And you'd make a lousy hobbit." I smirked to hide my uncertainty. When he did things like compliment me in a way that sounded suspiciously like flirting, and then kept going as if nothing happened, it was almost impossible to take my eyes off him.

Too bad I was so lousy at seeing the signs of someone's intent. Misread it one too many times in an ex.

"Are you kidding? I'd make the best fucking hobbit. First of all, look at the size of these feet. Legit thirteens right here." He raised his foot.

I bit back my *you know what they say about guys with big feet* comment. That visual was for me alone. "And you'd forgo adventure, to stay home in the Shire and live a peaceful life?"

"I wouldn't forgo it, but I would make sure we were back in time for afternoon tea." He cupped his hand to the side of his head, like he was covering an earpiece. "Alpha Echo Sierra, this is Foxtrot One Half. We're ten clicks out from Mount Doom. Over."

My giggles threatened to return. I loved Luke's impersonations. I couldn't do the voices like he could, but that rarely stopped me from participating. "This is Sierra One Half, on your three. We've got orcs inbound. Spinning up the guns. Over."

"I'm going in. Give me cover." He mimed holding onto something, then made a tossing gesture. "Ring is in the fire. I repeat, ring is in the fire. Tea's getting cold. Let's head out, boys." He straightened again. "See how much easier that would have been?"

I laughed. "Tolkien fans everywhere would have your hide."

"They'd need to get in line, behind the X fans we're about to piss off with this plot twist." Luke winked.

And here were the giggles. I couldn't stop them this time. It was like being drunk without alcohol. The harder I tried to rein them in, the more my body shook.

"It's not that funny." But Luke was laughing too.

waiting for it

Several minutes—and my aching sides and cheeks—later, we calmed down enough to stand upright again.

"Back to basics. The game is breaking on the call to the relationship AI." He spoke through gasps for breath, the occasional chuckle slipping through.

I composed myself and replied. "Are we passing too many variables? Not enough?" We'd asked the question before, in about fifty different ways. It wasn't the right direction to look in, but I was stuck on that point and couldn't move past it.

I could pretend there was no sexual tension between us better than he did. Even if he weren't my boss, I'd probably get stuck in the indecision of whether or not to say something to him.

My best friend, Sadie, would have made up her mind months ago and stuck to it. Either to pursue him or to ignore him. She was my exact opposite when it came to being outgoing and decisive. She'd landed her dream job because of it, along with two gorgeous boyfriends.

Yup. Two. And I couldn't even hold onto one for more than a couple of dates, because I was busy drooling over men I couldn't have and didn't dare approach.

"This is why you don't let programmers write romance," Luke said. "They think falling in love should be as simple as ticking the right 1s and 0s."

"*They* includes you." And me. While I didn't believe romance was truly that straightforward, there were a lot of days I wished it was. I'd love a checklist, telling me exactly what to do, say, and look for, so I'd know if I was spending time with the right person. Then again, *Do you work for him?* would have a big fat 1 next to it, telling me to back off.

Luke shook his head. "I wasn't born a geek. I'm not one of them."

"One of us."

"Not you. You're different."

My breath caught from the way he looked at me, holding me with that deep, seductive gaze. I shook the lust aside… mostly. "Because I have tits?"

"Because you don't think the way they do. You know we've got people on the team who won't be able to process this new storyline. Linear is great for programming from specs, but sometimes sucks for troubleshooting, and it definitely doesn't work for falling in love."

The game had a twist. A bigger one than we ever included. Fewer than ten of us had been told how all the pieces fit together. "That would explain the blue screen of death when The X finally takes off his mask for the first time."

waiting for it

Luke put one hand over his heart, took my hand with the other, and held my gaze. "Art"—his voice dropped an octave and addressed me with the one of the game character's names—"I have to tell you something. I… I…" He stopped, eyes wide and expression frozen.

"I know. I've always—" I struggled to stay in character and not smile, as I waved my hand in front of his face. "Are you listening?"

Luke didn't move.

He didn't so much as blink.

I snapped my fingers. "Hello?"

He finally focused on me. "Give me a plasma rifle in the 40-watt range," he said in a near-perfect Schwarzenegger-as-The-Terminator voice.

And now I was giggling again. I wouldn't let it get out of control. I wouldn't.

I managed to stop laughing long enough to talk. "All right, Romeo. If the problem is *us geeks* don't know how to write romance, how are you going to woo your in-game love interest?"

"Not Romeo. *Gomez.* As in *Adams.*"

Seriously? I raised my eyebrows. "And that's going to work for you?"

"Oh, *cara mia.*" Luke brushed a thumb over my knuckles.

A gasp rose in my throat. It was just a touch. Nothing special. Nothing more significant than he'd been doing all night.

"How long has it been since we waltzed?" As always, his accent was dead on. He tugged me from my spot at the end of his desk, spun us in a fluid circle, and dipped me.

Fucking *dipped me*, without dropping me. My giggle died when I saw the intensity in his gaze.

"I would die for you. I would kill for you. Either way, what bliss." He pressed his lips to mine.

The rest of the world vanished. *Whimper.*

Did I do that out loud?

I kissed him back. His lips were soft, but his mouth was hard and demanding, and crushed into mine while he straightened us.

He tightened his arm around my waist, and my body molded to his like they were meant to fit together. Each nibble across my lips and hungry swipe of his tongue made my pulse pound harder in my ears. Had I ever been kissed like this?

It didn't matter. At this moment, nothing else existed. I dragged my nails up his back, wanting to feel *everything.* His groan when he pressed into me, his erection digging into my hip, was as intoxicating as fine whiskey.

He pulled away and put some distance between us. "I'm sorry."

waiting for it

My heart skipped, tripped, and landed flat on its face. "For what? Kissing me?" There was no way to keep from sounding hurt. I didn't just read a kiss wrong, did I?

"No. Definitely not." Luke reached for me but dropped his hand. "But I'm your boss. That's it. I quit."

I was typically pretty quick on the uptake, but my brain was struggling to keep track of this conversation. Maybe because that kiss had forced all the blood from my brain into every single extremity that could tingle with desire. "You can't get out of this project that easily." My laugh sounded as forced as it was.

"You were willing to sell your soul to Sauron to finish it."

"That's my soul. I'm not using it for much else, and these hours mean we're already the walking dead. But you're talking about—" his career. How did we go from fantasy kisses and dancing to this? I was taking things too seriously. Why did I always do that? I should have laughed off the *I quit* joke and gotten back to work like nothing happened.

Except Luke didn't look upset. Not with me. He was still watching me with those dark eyes that made my brain turn to mush. "Every time you laugh or sigh or say… anything—" He shook his head and let out a long breath. "This is so inappropriate."

"Yeah. Totally." I knew that. Or I might have, if it were happening with anyone besides Luke.

"I never want you to think you're in this job because of anything other than your skill, or that you have to do anything other than your work, to stay employed here."

Right. Because *sleep with me or I'll fire you* was a thing. I couldn't imagine Luke doing that, which was a good reason for me to be wary of it. I could imagine him doing a lot of other things to me, though I usually tried to keep those thoughts to a minimum. Getting work done would be infinitely harder if I actually let the fantasies run rampant—of him pinning me to the wall and kissing along my neck… my chest… lower…

"Anne?" He studied me with concern.

I didn't want to pretend the attraction didn't flow both ways. If work weren't an obstacle, would things go further?

What would Sadie do?

I didn't know.

Don't I?

Okay, I did, because Sadie and I might as well be twins, for as close as we'd been since we were kids.

waiting for it

"What if we pretended?" My voice cracked on the question.

"Pretended… I wasn't your boss?"

Chapter Two

My heart was throwing itself against my ribs like it was in a one-man cage match, and I couldn't find my voice. I nodded.

"Strangers, then?" Luke stepped within arm's reach. "Random encounter? Undeniable chemistry? Two people who're definitely not us, even though we look and think exactly the same, who can't keep their hands off each other?" His voice rumbled over me with temptation.

Being picked up by him in a bar? Or anywhere? Yeah, that was hot. "Something like that." My response came out raspy.

He took my hand again and led me away from the desk. When we reached the small table at the other end of his office, he spun to face me. The toes of his shoes touched mine, and if I leaned in, our lips would meet.

"What's a nice place like you doing in a girl like this?" he asked.

I laughed at the Deadpool reference. If he was pretending to be a stranger, he had a pretty good knack for getting into my head. "I'd quote the movie back at you, but even if we're pretending we don't work here, Rinslet can't afford the copyright lawsuit."

Luke's throaty chuckle rolled over me. "Let's skip the pick-up lines," he said. "I'm not great at those anyway. How about we fast-forward to the part where I invite you back to my room?"

"Yes." *Fucking yes.* My voice had recovered.

He slid a hand to the back of my neck and kissed me again. There was no easing into this. He crushed against my mouth with an intensity I shared, and I parted my lips, to deepen the kiss.

Our tongues danced and thrashed against each other. He drew me closer, but I wanted to feel more than the pressure of his frame against mine; I wanted to be part of him.

I pushed his shirt up. One of us groaned—or was that both of us?—when my fingers met his bare skin.

His scent mingled with the faint musk of desire plus a full day's work. Everything about this, about us, was distinct and hyper-real. The way he tangled his fingers in my hair and tugged. The glide of his mouth along my jaw and to my collarbone. The barely-there fuzz of hair, when I slid my fingers up his torso and dug them into his chest, looking for something to hold onto.

"You're fucking incredible," Luke murmured against my shoulder, and the words vibrated through me. "I want to strip you down, and lick your pussy until you're grinding against my face and writhing in ecstasy. I bet you taste like peaches."

And he was a dirty talker. From the increased throb between my legs, apparently that was a turn-on.

The chime of his cell phone, unnaturally loud amid our panting and moaning, shattered the mood.

"I should get that," Luke said breathlessly.

"Right." I didn't know if I was hurt he didn't ignore it, or relieved he chose to answer.

As he crossed the room, cool air sank into my cheeks and pushed away the heat of fantasy.

I brushed my fingers over my tingling lips. The flesh was tender and swollen. My pulse wouldn't stop doing speed-trial laps. What the fuck was I doing? Was I really going to sleep with my boss?

Yeah, as far as bosses went, Luke was... *wow*, but I had to look him in the eye every day. Lust was one thing, but acting on it? Going further would be a mistake. I was a master of bad decisions, and that one would top the list.

"Sorry about that." He returned but kept his distance.

waiting for it

Good. It was. Really. I just needed *all* of me to be glad he wasn't close enough to touch. I wouldn't even ask what the apology was for—the interruption or what came before. "No worries. I think we should call it a night soon, anyway."

A shadow crossed his face, but it was gone before I could identify it. "You're right. It's late. Our brains are stuck in a debug loop."

"That's it." I knew what the issue was with the code. Thank God, because it pushed the awkwardness out of my thoughts for a few seconds. "Check this out." I strode back to the white board, erased several of the lines in his flow chart, and drew in new ones. Not an easy trick while my brain was trying to remember if I knew any positions in the Kama Sutra. "This routine is stuck in a loop."

"You're right." He moved to stand behind me but kept a couple feet between us.

A couple feet of gaping chasm.

I ignored the thought and kept drawing. "We need to call this variable sooner and populate it at a higher level, so these modules can access it."

"Brilliant. If I'd know I had magic lips, I'd have done— *Brilliant.*"

My cheeks were burning again, but not from desire this time. *Done that sooner.* I knew what he wanted to say, because I was itching to joke that, *if your kisses come with programmer mojo, we need to do that more often.*

Not an option. I needed to relegate tonight's make-out session to storage, no matter how incredibly delicious and tempting his kisses were… How much I'd enjoyed his hands roaming my body—

"I'll get my team started on this in the morning. Which means we're done for the night." My words tumbled out in a rush.

"Smart thinking. We both need sleep." Was he looking at me funny? I couldn't bear to check. "Good work today." His tone was strained.

You too. You're an amazing kisser. "Thanks."

"Walk you to your car?"

"Sure." I had to accept. We always walked out to the parking lot together during late nights. He insisted it was to keep me safe, and I liked the idea of him looking out for me.

I grabbed my laptop—not that I would do any work between tonight and tomorrow morning, but just in case—and waited for Luke at the elevator.

The silence we rode downstairs in was deafening.

As we stepped into the parking garage, he coughed to clear his throat. "Anne…"

"Yeah?" I didn't pause in my stride or look at him. I couldn't.

waiting for it

He loosely grabbed my wrist, and a fresh shock of desire sped through me as he spun me to face him. "I don't regret what happened up there. I probably should, but I'm not sorry for kissing you."

"Okay." So not intelligent. "Me too." Only mildly better.

The corners of his mouth tugged up. His half-smile was as sexy as everything else he did. "But you're also one of the best employees I've ever had. And I'm not saying that because you've got incredible lips. You're one of my best hiring decisions."

"Thank you. I like working for you too. You're a good boss." The praise flushed me, but I could focus on the work parts of it and become a functionally vocal person again. I tugged free from his grip and kept walking. "Which is why I'm glad we stopped."

"Sure." He didn't sound convinced. "But it doesn't change anything else between us. I can't have this awkwardness. We need to be all right."

Easier said than done. "We're fine."

"Anne?" The *I call bullshit* was clear in his tone.

I should have assured him with more conviction.

We reached my car. I was both grateful and disappointed for the excuse to cut the conversation short. "We'll be fine. I just need some sleep."

"Okay. 'Night Anne."

I gave him one last glance. The lighting down here was harsh—bright in some spots, dark in others to cast deep shadows, and a nasty shade of yellow—but he still looked amazing. Sympathetic, concerned, and fuckable, all at the same time.

"Night," I said.

As soon as I hit the main road, I cranked my radio and cracked my window to let the cold air hit my face.

None of it erased the repeat in my head. The memory of making out with Luke like we were horny teenagers alternated between ending the way it had in his office and continuing as though we hadn't been interrupted.

By the time I got home, my body was on fire with fantasy fed by memory.

I made it inside, and locked the door behind me. I'd purchased it when I started making good money, right as the market crashed, because I'd been convinced property was a good investment. Turned out my ex just wanted a bigger place I was paying for and he was crashing in.

. There were days when living in this big a house by myself felt lonely. Tonight I didn't mind

waiting for it

the rambling house. The solitude meant I didn't have to worry about anyone walking in on me.

Sparks of desire danced under my skin, prompted by the images in my head of Luke gliding his palm up my chest, to tease me through my bra. My nipples, still rock hard, strained against cotton, begging for attention.

I dropped my laptop by the front door and stripped off my shirt, letting my hands roam where Luke's did in my head. To tug down the cups of my bra and free my breasts. To knead, and pinch and tug.

The pleasure that spilled through me was different than me just feeling myself up. It was fueled by whispers of *him*. What if he'd come home with me?

I backed myself to the wall at the fantasy of both of us being too eager to wait.

He'd press into my body again, him dressed, me half-stripped down. Would he be gentle? God, I hoped not.

I swore I could feel his hungry kisses, devouring me. Gliding down my neck. Alternating with playful nips and the occasional hard bite. Sucking on my nipples until I squirmed at the attention.

In my mind, we fumbled with each other's zipper, not wanting to break away from the kissing and exploration to give the task proper attention. In reality, I'd have to undo my own jeans.

When I wrapped my fingers around his shaft, his groan echoed in my ear. It was the kind of sound that said, *I'm tired of ignoring this.*

He'd shove my bottoms down as far as possible without breaking any other contact, and dip his fingers between my legs.

I mimicked the motion, and my body jerked at the new touch. I'd prefer his hand, but wrapped in fantasy, mine would do. I was already wet and slick, thanks to a night of better-than-should-be-allowed making out.

In my head, we were impatient. There was no more time for seduction. I stroked along my slit, dipping near my opening and then away, the way I wanted him to. My senses were screaming for relief, and my breath came in short gasps.

I honed in on my clit, sliding my fingers on either side and stroking. Orgasm built inside but didn't grant me relief.

Was I whimpering out loud?

I worked myself harder. Faster. The images in my head bled into the physical, until everything was a blur, except the sharp, disparate focus of my need.

Come for me, Anne. I swore I heard his voice in my ear and felt the playful sting of teeth biting the lobe.

waiting for it

Climax spilled through me, yanking a cry from my throat and shuddering over me.

I kept up the frantic self-attention until I was too sensitive and jerking away from my own touch.

Another gasp escaped when I rested fully against the wall. My legs were wobbly. I bet they'd be more so if Luke was here.

I sank to the ground, and the cold entryway tile bit into my ass.

I'd never dared entertain these thoughts before. Not consciously. Sure, my dreams betrayed me sometimes, and Luke visited me in them. But *letting* myself think about being with him gave the idea more shape and weight than it should have.

Heat still flooded me. I'd linger in the afterglow a little longer.

And hope post-coital bliss numbed the pit in my heart that reminded me this could only ever be a dream.

Chapter Three

Hangovers had never been an issue for me. I could hold my liquor with the best of them, and had drunk my friends under the table more than once.

But as I got ready for work, my eyes burned in protest of being open, my skull throbbed, and my mouth felt like I'd slept with cotton stuffed in it. I could stand to sleep for another fifty years.

Which meant never seeing my friends again. And surrendering my dream of moving into a Director position similar to Luke's. That would suck. It also meant not working with Luke anymore. That would save me a lot of awkwardness… but it would also suck.

I shook aside the darkish gray thoughts and got ready for work. I wasn't running late according to office time, but I was for me. I liked to get there by seven thirty, because it gave me time to settle into the day before anyone else showed up.

Was last night a mistake? Obvious answer was *yes*, but every time I brushed something across my lips—my fingers, the toothbrush, lip gloss—I swore

waiting for it

I still felt Luke. And now we could never do that again.

Was it really better to have made out and lost than never to have made out at all?

Depended on how the next few weeks of fumbling through, pretending nothing happened, went.

That should have been the last of those thoughts, but no, variations on the same repeated my entire drive to work, and when I settled into my desk, I was treated to the sequel.

No new email should have come in between last night and this morning, so I let my computer load while I went to fetch coffee from the break room. If I ventured to the cafeteria downstairs, I could get extra espresso and more sugar than should be possible in a single drink, but that meant facing other people. I wasn't quite ready for that yet.

When I got back to my desk, there was an email from Luke. Just his name made my heart do a funny dance, set to the Final Fantasy battle music. I needed to get that under control. How long could I hide in my office before anyone wanted face-to-face interaction?

According to Luke's email, another thirty-seven minutes. *Mandatory team meeting. Bullpen. 8:30.*

Hurrah.

There was another email from Mike, my counterpart in our Sacramento office. I didn't always care for him, but I respected his work ethic, considering it was an hour earlier there.

You didn't get those files delivered that you promised. Waiting since last week.

Yeah, I didn't care for him at all, especially since he'd copied Luke in a way that felt like *I'm telling the boss on you.*

I forwarded him the message in question, that I'd sent when I said I would, with my nauseatingly polite *Here you go. You must have missed this.*

His reply came in seconds later. *I didn't miss it. You didn't send it before.*

I bit the inside of my cheek. If I didn't have proof, I might believe him that I hadn't done it. That I remembered wrong. Thank God for *Sent Mail* history.

As people trickled in for the day, some of them waving as they passed my open office door, and others engrossed in their phones, I had zero focus.

Get it under control, me. I have work to do.

At 8:24, Chase knocked on my door. "Any idea what this is about?" he asked.

"Nope."

"Interesting. Let's go find out." He gestured toward the Bullpen.

waiting for it

Chase was Sadie's older brother, and by proxy as good as my stepbrother—the sexy kind of stepbrother, people wrote romance novels about. If I hadn't basically grown up in their house, I'd let myself pay more attention to how attractive he was. Dark hair, the same pale-blue eyes Sadie had, and the perfect amount of muscle in his arms to dip a girl and kiss her.

I might be fooling everyone else, but I couldn't lie to myself. I knew exactly how sexy Chase was, and unlike with Luke, I didn't pretend the fantasies didn't exist. I'd been daydreaming about Chase longer than I understood what the pulsing need between my thighs meant, when I thought about him kissing me.

And now last night with Luke was back in my head, overlapping my Chase repository like a scorching double exposure.

I gently tucked it all aside and fell into step beside Chase. He worked in Sales, not Development, but he was part of our team because he'd sold merchandising rights to several companies, for the game we were currently behind on. He had as much of a stake in the game hitting market as any of us did.

We took a spot near the *front* of the area we called *Bullpen*. It was an empty space amid the cubicles, near the windows, where we would set up gaming parties, pizza days, or whatever required a little extra space.

Including stand-up meetings.

"Where's the boss?" Chase whispered, when the clock ticked past 8:30.

I shrugged. Good question. Luke was never late.

When he finally stepped in front of the group a couple minutes later, his brow was pinched and his lips drawn in a thin line. A smile flickered across his face when he glanced at me.

My stomach did little a series of little flip flops.

"Someone looks like they've been force fed shit this morning," Chase muttered.

Luke's glare said Chase hadn't been as quiet as he'd intended.

"Sorry for being late. I was talking to Zach." Luke's voice carried across the room without a problem, and all the chatter stopped. Zach was one of the two company owners, and not the one who usually dealt with developers. If he was taking up Luke's time, odds were it included bad news.

"This won't take long," Luke said. "You know I'm always as direct with you as I can be. *Full transparency* and all that."

And now the flips in my stomach had turned into gnawing edges of tension. Something was

waiting for it

wrong, and Luke hadn't been able to stop it. I rarely saw him like this, but when I did, he never had good news.

He always went to bat for us with management, but some things couldn't be diminished or erased. How badly this launch had gone, for instance.

Luke scrubbed his face. "I know crunch has been hard on everyone, but I have to ask you to hold on a little longer."

In the history of the company, this was the first time employees had been asked to do something like put in sixty- to eighty-hour weeks, for months on end, to meet a deadline. In the past, a couple of days at a time or an extra weekend here and there was the most anyone saw. The overtime was voluntary and paid, but our team was so invested in this game, we'd all agreed.

Rinslet was careful with their launch dates. They never made one public until they were ready to release, because they refused to miss a launch. This game was done six months ago. Everyone had signed off, alpha and beta tests were solid, and we were ready to go. And then everything fell apart. QA started failing. User acceptance testing. They were minor issues at first, but with each problem we fixed, more of the game broke.

Chase raised his hand. Which—okay? This wasn't that kind of an environment, and he'd never been a *wait for my turn to talk* kind of person.

I didn't think it was possible, but Luke's expression grew darker. "Hughes."

"Your people are the best"—Chase nudged me lightly—"but my programming skills aren't going to make anything better for anyone. What do you need me to do?"

Sell the big bosses on going easy on us?

Luke sighed. "That's where full transparency comes in. Management is watching us closely. If we don't get this right, other people may be brought in to help."

"And that's... bad?" I could spin up another dozen developers in a day, and more staff would be wonderful.

Chase tensed. I actually felt the slight tremor where his arm rested against mine. "*Help* to fill the gap left by anyone who won't be here."

A wave of murmurs rolled through the room. Rinslet was going to fire people if we didn't pull this off. Most likely starting with Luke and me, since we were overseeing development.

"Are you threatening us?" someone else asked.

Luke shook his head. "No. I'm telling you the way things are. I can't guarantee jobs—yours, mine, anyone's—if we miss this new deadline."

waiting for it

Here in Salt Lake City, there were only two big game developers—Rinslet and Digital Media— and working for DM meant full-time crunch and a lot less understanding from management.

I didn't want to find a new job. I liked working here. With good bosses and great benefits. With Luke. With Chase.

Losing my job was definitely more terrifying than whether or not I had someone fun and sexy to watch during meetings.

My lips tingled with a ghost of a memory of Luke's kisses and the intensity in his. It was going to take a while to pretend I didn't want that again.

"I have faith in you guys." The strength and confidence were back in Luke's voice. "You're going to rock this release. Back to work, and remember to clock all overtime."

The meeting broke up, and I headed back to my office, Chase walking next to me.

"I'm guessing this means you don't have time for lunch," he said.

I gave him a look I hoped properly conveyed *are you fucking kidding me?* I was considering tossing a cot in the corner, so I didn't have to waste time commuting. Going out to lunch was a luxury I couldn't afford.

He gave me a dry half-smile. "I'll bring you some General Tsao's?"

"That would be amazing." I'd made him grovel for what he did to Sadie, but she'd forgiven him and so did I. Which was good, because I hated being mad at him.

He squeezed my arm. "See you in a few hours. You've got this."

What would it be like, to have as much faith in our ability to deliver as Chase and Luke seemed to?

He left, and I dove back into work. I shut out the rest of the world and focused on code. We'd moved past the *fingers flying over keys* stage, and were in the *stare at the screen and see why things were break*ing point.

A knock on my door startled me. I looked up, to see Chase holding a bag from our favorite Chinese place.

"Sorry I'm late." He crossed the room to hand me the food.

I glanced at my clock. Almost one-thirty. Talk about losing track of time. My stomach grumbled at the scent of food. "I didn't notice, so no worries" I took the bag, resisting the urge to tear into it and eat like an animal. I shouldn't have skipped breakfast. "You're the best. Thank you."

"Anytime. Really. You want dinner, too?"

"We're having pizza brought in." Luke's comment made me jump for the second time in as

waiting for it

many minutes. He stepped into my office. "I need to talk to you for a minute."

I swore I could smell his cologne from here. I couldn't really, but my brain was bent on convincing me otherwise. My thoughts ran rampant with memories, and my skin heated everywhere he'd touched last night.

I wasn't ready for one-on-one time in a closed space. Not yet. How were we supposed to pretend nothing had happened?

Chapter Four

I nodded at Chase, to imply I was in the middle of another conversation. "Can it wait just a few?"

"It won't take long, and it's not top secret or anything. He can stay if he wants."

Was it weird that Luke wouldn't look directly at Chase, or was I searching for a distraction, outside of the way my body was screaming to be closer to Luke?

Door was open. We had witnesses. I could rein in my imagination under these circumstances.

Unless Chase wants to join us.

What the fuck, brain? No. I was *not* going down that path. "What's up?" At least I could still speak normally, even if my thoughts were trying to sabotage my composure on every level.

"You and I are heading to Sacramento tomorrow, to meet face to face with Team Percival."

"Hey, me too," Chase said. "I have a vendor out there I need to play nice with."

waiting for it

This trip wasn't happening for me. And not only because I wasn't ready for that much alone time with Luke. "I can't go with you. I have too much work." We were behind, and I was going to fly off to the other offices for what? A friendly visit? Besides, Mike already thought I was trying to overshadow him. No reason to get in his face about it.

"I need you there." The undercurrent in Luke's tone sent pleasant shivers up my spine. "Give me specific concerns and let me address them."

I have too much work to do felt pretty specific to me. "It doesn't matter that it's a short flight. Once you factor in travel, boarding, security, any delays, we've wasted at least half a day each way. And only some of that time can be used for work. Why aren't we doing this via video? In fact, why am I involved at all, beyond the usual coordination?" Not that I minded the sound of Luke, saying *I need you.*

"Scott and I have some concerns about Mike, and I want you there as a second opinion, while we immerse ourselves in their culture."

Scott was the other owner, and the genius behind Rinslet's early tech.

I knew exactly what Luke was talking about. I had concerns about Mike's behavior too—though that didn't always mean anything in my case. And the more I thought about it, the less I wanted to turn down a trip with Luke, even if it was all business.

But I really did have too much work. "Mike's going to be on his best behavior if upper management is in the office."

"Some things can't be hidden, especially if they're a part of his everyday business," Chase said.

Luke raised his eyebrows. "Did you just back me up?"

Why was he surprised? Chase was outspoken but not argumentative.

"Don't get used to it." The sudden edge in Chase's voice caught me off guard.

Was there some sort of tension between the two of them I never noticed before? Who the hell knew? I hadn't even wanted to admit until last night that Luke's flirting meant anything.

And now that I knew, I couldn't use that information to my advantage.

Back to business. "I don't really have a choice, do I?" I asked.

"You always have a choice. I'd rather have you with me for this, but you get final say." Luke sounded sincere.

"I guess I'll go." I let out an exaggerated sigh. We had too much work, for this to be any sort of vacation, but I didn't want to let him down, and I

waiting for it

was having a hard time remembering we should keep some distance between us.

Luke's smile was warm enough to make my pulse skip. "Thank you," he said. "I'll have Jamie make reservations. Expect to fly out tomorrow. I'll let you eat." He gave me one final glance and was gone.

"Is something weird between you two?" Chase stole the question I meant to ask him.

There was no way I was giving him an honest answer. "No. Why do you say that?"

"No reason. Just curious. Eat your food before it gets cold, Annie."

No one was allowed to call me that, except him. I had no idea why I let him get away with it, but the way he said *Annie* always made me smile. "I'm waiting until you leave, so I'm not rudely eating in front of you."

"And once I go, you'll forget for the next two hours. Eat." He knew me too well.

I set up my food on the corner of my desk and took a bite. The spicy-sweet of General Tsao's chicken washed over my tongue, and my stomach grumbled in appreciation. I shoved another forkful into my mouth quickly.

"How's development going?" Chase asked.

I stared at him, eyebrows raised and mouth full of food.

He laughed. "Sorry."

"No you're not," I said around my food. I chewed, swallowed, and washed it down with a swig of Coke. He'd even brought me the bottled kind with real sugar. He was too good to me. "Latest bug is that things are freezing right before… things." I wasn't supposed to share that detail.

"The big plot twist, right? If I beg and look pretty, will you tell me?"

I never had before, though it was silly to keep it from Chase. *Tell no one* meant *tell no one*. "Nope. But I'll give you a hint. It does have to do with the big confession of love."

"You sure you guys didn't write it that way? To freeze right before the good stuff, I mean," he teased.

I twisted my mouth in mock frustration. "You sound like Luke."

"You take that back." There was no power in his retort. "In fact, I bet when he said it, he did so in some sort of bad accent."

"It was a perfect accent." My reply came out more defensive than I intended, and I took another bite of food, letting the heat from the spice distract me so my mind didn't pick the situation apart.

"I accept that."

"If you want me to eat, you tell me about your day, so I can," I said.

waiting for it

Chase looked up for a moment. before focusing on me again. "Staff meeting this morning. Yoshi was in office."

My *oh?* came out muffled. Yoshi was VP of Sales and Marketing, which meant he was Chase and Jax's boss. Everyone had a story about him, in a good way. He was quirky, like so many of us, but he was as kind and genuine as anyone.

"Jax is supposed to be drilling down on a new merchandising contract, and none of us knows Yoshi is going to be there. He walks in five minutes into things, and everyone stops. He must have some sort of announcement or something important to share, right?"

I shrugged in agreement. Usually when a big boss crashed a meeting that was the case.

"He doesn't want a seat at the table," Chase said. "Instead he sits in one of the chairs against the wall, and sets a Taco Bell bag next to him. Everyone's staring and waiting for him to say something, and he's digging into a Chalupa. He looks up, mouth full, and says, *Don't let me interrupt.*"

"I bet Jax appreciated that," I said sarcastically. Jax had been negotiating this contract for months.

Chase grinned. "He cranked the cheer and enthusiasm to eleven."

"Extra irritated," I said in understanding.

"So Jax falls back into it. He's explaining how we're going to do a *Console Power Magazine* tie-in, and Yoshi asks, *What does this look like?* He's holding up a burrito."

There was a punchline in here, and knowing Yoshi, it would be a pun. I preferred the stories second hand, because Chase had better timing, and I loved watching him—well—do anything. "And Jax said *a burrito?*"

Chase nodded. "Yoshi can't stop smirking. He says, *A baby donkey.*"

A little burro? I groaned at the bad pun, but I was also laughing. "Worst one this week."

"Worst one I've told you about. I save you from the really bad ones."

"You're such a gentleman."

He tapped me playfully on the nose. "I absolutely am. I'm going to let you work, now that you've eaten. See you tomorrow?"

"See you tomorrow."

After Chase left, the amusement he'd brought faded quickly. I tried to concentrate on code. Exhaustion, food coma, and lust wanted me to daydream about either Luke or Chase instead. Or both together. Sleep-deprived me lacked a few filters. I had less than a day to get the potent desire

waiting for it

out of my system and go back to the passive attraction.

I forced my gaze to my screen. The focus lasted about five minutes, before Luke knocked.

"Do you have a minute?" This time he stepped into my office and closed the door behind him.

No. The refusal froze in my throat. My insides twisted, and my brain grasped how intimately small my office was when the door was closed. How had I never noticed that before?

It only took him a couple of steps to move to the side of my desk. There was no furniture barrier now. "I want to make sure things are all right between us." His voice was low.

This wasn't exactly a private place to talk, even closed off from the office. "Fine." I needed to keep my answers vague. "I just had to—"

"Get home. Yeah. I meant everything I said."

That he was willing to quit his job to kiss me? That we couldn't continue what we'd been doing? That he imagined I tasted like peaches? "That's a lot of conflicting information."

"It's all true. I know what I'm saying. If you weren't under me—" His wince matched my mental one. Did he just get the same image I did? "Things are the way they are, and none of what happened has an impact on your job."

So he kept insisting, but it very much did. I'd never look at him the same way again. I wasn't saying that out loud, especially not here. If I was more like Sadie, would I stop thinking about this, and act?

I was me, though. "Good to know."

"Then we're all right? I don't have to worry about you hiding from me, or anything?" The lightheartedness in his question was strained.

I forced a smile. "Yup. Things are great."

He raised an eyebrow. "I'll take that for now."

As he left, I sank a few inches in my chair. Things would get back to normal between us. It would take time some time, though.

Did I want my relationship with Luke to go back to the way it was?

It didn't matter what I wanted. Returning to pretending it wasn't him was the only choice I had.

Chapter Five

After another night of working past ten, this time isolated in my office, and with an entire floor of developers between me and Luke, morning came too soon.

Taking a seven o'clock flight should get us into the Sacramento offices by about ten, which only meant a few hours of missed work. Still time I dreaded not having, almost as much as I missed the sleep I wouldn't be getting anytime soon.

At least I could dress in comfortable clothes, rather than business attire. Our company dress code was basically *clean, and make sure your genitals don't hang out.*

I sleepwalked my way through a quick shower, checking in online for my flight, and doing one last inventory of what I'd packed.

All set.

My phone buzzed with a new text.

I'm here. It was Lyn, my other best friend, who was dropping me off at the airport.

She'd been Sadie's friend first, and when the two of them met, I didn't know what to think of Lyn. She had that Sadie-confidence I envied, but something less self-assured hid underneath, and back then, I didn't know if I was jealous of her for covering up the insecurity, or hated her for not owning it like I did.

Lyn and I had moved past that, partly thanks to a little *experimenting*, that was physically incredible but emotionally didn't have the spark either of us wanted. Now, I was glad for her friendship.

Speaking of—if Lyn and I worked things out, Luke and I could still be friends too, right? Except my heart didn't want Lyn, and I was pretty sure it was interested in more from Luke.

I grabbed my suitcase, laptop, and purse, gave the house one last look—not that I'd spent enough time here in the last few months to miss the place— and headed out to her small SUV. After setting my luggage in the back, I joined her up front.

"I brought you a present," Lyn said in a sing-song tone as she held up a coffee cup.

I kissed her noisily on the cheek, and took the drink as I dropped into my seat. "My hero." The coffee scalded just a little going down, and left the burn of extra sweet in its wake. "Perfect."

"How's work?" Lyn pointed us toward the airport.

waiting for it

I made out with my boss two nights ago. You know—Luke, the hot one—and now I can't stop thinking about fucking him. I wanted to spill everything, but I needed to wrap my brain around it first. "It's work. How 'bout you?"

She drummed her fingers rapidly against the steering wheel and let out a subdued but happy squeal. "So, you know how I was talking to Roxie?"

I rolled the name in my brain until I made a match—names weren't my specialty. "The podcaster Sadie knows?"

"That's her. She came by the café yesterday, and she loves it. She's going to have me on her show, because—and I quote—*everyone needs to know about this place.*"

That was a happier wake-up call than the coffee. "*Yay.*" I clapped as best I could with a cup in my hand. "Tell me when, and I'll make the whole office listen."

Lyn twisted her mouth. "That won't be necessary, but you can listen and tell me how awesome I am."

"Duh." I was excited for the news.

Lyn owned a gaming and anime café called *Loading Java*. For a long time, she'd only spent what the business could afford, to keep it open. But almost a year ago, she took out a loan to expand. Business slumped off right after, and she struggled to stay in the black since. Christmas rush helped. A shout-out from a gaming podcaster with a huge platform could help even more.

We chatted about other random things while she drove. The airport was less than fifteen miles from my place, and this early in the morning, there was no traffic. Before I knew it, she was pulling up to the drop-off curb.

"Thank you for the ride," I said as I hopped out.

"Anytime. Try to have a little fun if you can, and text us when you land."

Us being her and Sadie. Thanks to a shitty home life when I was younger and my having severed all ties to my blood relations, Lyn, Sadie, Chase, Jax, and Grayson were my family.

I grabbed my bags from the back of her car and headed inside. It was the middle of the week, so the only people here were other business travelers. Going through security was fast and painless, aside from the fact they made me guzzle my coffee or I'd have to throw it away. Within a few minutes, I was heading through the terminal toward my gate.

My feet slowed when Luke came into view. He was leaning against a pillar, flipping through his phone, looking as gorgeous in profile as any other time. The flutters in my stomach spread, dancing

waiting for it

across my skin, tingling in my lips, and lingering every place he'd touched or kissed.

When he looked up and flashed me a lazy smile, it was tempting to swoon and faint away.

This had to stop. As much as part of me didn't want to ignore what happened, I had to, or I'd never get any work done again.

I waved back and joined him at the edge of the gate waiting area.

The corners of his eyes crinkled when his smile grew. Did they always do that? *God*, I was screwed if he was even cuter than I'd realized. "Smart thinking, grabbing coffee here," I nodded at his cup.

"You could do the same," he said.

"Probably not a good idea. Lyn hooked me up, but I couldn't bring it past security so I chugged it."

Luke winced. "I don't know if I should be sympathetic or impressed."

He knew my friends. Both Sadie and Lyn had been my *dates* for various company functions and parties. I didn't care for the big gatherings, so they made sure I put in my time.

Silence lulled between us. That was normal. We'd known each other for years. So why was I staring at my shoes and thinking of excuses to walk away?

"What kind of a seat did you get? On the plane?" Luke asked.

I hadn't checked. Where did I put my phone?

Luke laughed lightly. "Stop, Anne. Front pocket?"

"Oh, right." I angled said pocket toward him. When his fingers brushed my hip through denim, I sucked in a sharp breath through my teeth.

His lip twitched, but he didn't pause, extracting my phone and unlocking it.

This wasn't normal, was it? Most people didn't let their friends and significant others have their phone lock screen codes, let alone their bosses. Why had that never occurred to me before now?

He raised his brows as he stared at the screen. "5A."

"Are we next to each other?" Could I spend an hour and a half next to him on a plane? Of course I could. Best time to practice acting normal. And sitting in cramped seats, arms pressed together, fingers itching to intertwine—

"No. *Someone*"—he gave me a curious look—"got an upgrade to business class."

Oh. "Thank you."

"For what?"

"Your assistant made the reservations?" Speaking of which—Luke could have told me he'd

waiting for it

gotten me the upgrade, rather than going through all this… whatever it was.

"Then she likes you more than me. I didn't tell her to do that." He slipped my phone back in my pocket. "I kind of wish I'd thought of it, but enjoy the seat. Think of it as a spot of good luck, which you deserve."

"Thanks." And now there was going to be awkward silence again. "So I've been thinking about the configuration of the inventory call stack." Technical work-talk—guaranteed to make any lull in conversation that much more boring.

He placed a finger under my chin and tilted my head up.

My breath caught. My mind froze. A tingle raced across my lips, and I resisted the urge to lick it away.

"We're not going to fix the game today. When was the last time you had a chance to read or watch something new? Take advantage of the next few hours of freedom," Luke said.

My tongue flicked across my bottom lip before I realized what I was doing. Could he hear my heart hammering against my ribs?

"Okay." I couldn't pull my gaze from his. Would he kiss me again? Bad idea anyway, but in the middle of the airport, when Chase could show up any minute? "I'll pretend to relax." I tried to act natural about moving out of arm's reach.

"Ladies and gentlemen, we're ready to begin boarding." A voice came over the loudspeaker and announced that they were now boarding Business Class rows.

Luke waved a hand toward the boarding ramp. "Go. Enjoy the leg room and amenities."

"If I have to." I gave an exaggerated sigh, accompanied by a smile.

I boarded, stowed my carry-on, and settled into my seat. I was in the last row before the curtain that separated our seats from coach. Who would be next to me? I wasn't up for small talk on the best days, and especially not first thing in the morning, on a flight I'd been reluctant to take.

Read. Interesting idea. Pulled up my books on my phone. Biggest problem—where to start. It had been way too long since I lost myself in a book.

I was torn between looking engrossed if someone sat next to me, and watching for Luke to pass by, without looking like I was watching. I'd scrolled through the first fifty or so books on my to-be-read list half a dozen times, before I realized I wasn't registering any of the titles.

One of the attendants announced they were getting ready to close the doors. No one had taken the seat next to me. My luck was even better this

waiting for it

morning than I'd expected. I turned my attention back to my phone. What to read?

Someone brushed my arm, and a familiar clean scent teased me. It was like Luke's, but not quite. I looked up, to see Chase sliding into the seat next to me. Wait. Did Chase and Luke wear the same cologne? How had I never noticed that before?

"Nice of you to finally show up," I said playfully.

"It's all about making an entrance." He settled quickly and turned to halfway face me. "Glad you got my present."

His…? "The seat upgrade?"

"Yup. I figure you're overworked and don't want to be here, and I had the points. You might as well enjoy this a little."

What was it, with everyone telling me that today? "It's a perfect fit. Thank you."

Some of the tension drained from my neck, as I sank into my seat. Chase sitting next to me was pretty much Ideal Scenario Number One. He'd understand if I didn't want to talk. The silence between us wouldn't feel awkward. He'd be a perfect buffer. This trip was shaping up to be pretty decent after all.

"So what's up with you and Luke?" Chase's tone was casual. The plane pulled from the gate and headed toward the runway.

I choked on the air. "Nothing." My answer came out in a single syllable. I drew a deep breath. *Slow down.* "I mean, why would you think…? Nothing's up." I managed to enunciate every word.

"Mhm. Then you need to get that blushing thing under control."

I pressed my palms into my flaming cheeks. "I'm not blushing." Was I?

"Every time you see him or hear his name, since yesterday morning."

Fuck. I slid my hands to cover my entire face. Who else had noticed? No one, right? Chase simply knew me that well. "It was just a kiss." Or two. Or more. And a lot of groping. "And we're pretending it didn't happen." My already quiet words were muffled by my hands.

The plane started moving again, but I was too focused on Chase's lack of response. I glanced sideways at him.

His expression unreadable.

"What?" I asked.

He shrugged. "If you were looking to hook up with someone in the office, you could have come to me." He trailed a finger lightly along my jaw.

My breath caught, and my pulse hammered in my ears. "We didn't *hook up*." I wanted to laugh his words off as a joke, but *God* if he didn't summon

waiting for it

every fantasy I'd ever had about Chase at once. "You? Really?"

"Ouch. Or anyone but him. But yes, me."

The plane lifted off. Chase tilted his head and brushed his lips over mine.

The bottom dropped out of my everything.

Chapter Six

The pressure from the plane ascending combined with the surprise of Chase's kiss, squeezing my heart and fracturing the wall I didn't realize I'd built there to keep him out. The clenching was exquisite and startling.

I didn't know how to react. What to think, beyond *this is incredible*.

He broke the kiss, then dipped in for another and a quick peck, before finally pulling away. The intensity of his gaze sent another wave of fissures racing along the box around my heart.

"Annie? Say something." Chase's tone was a sweetly shadowed blend of command and concern.

"Me?" The question slipped out as my reality swarmed back into my thoughts. "You want *me* to say something." I processed his words. "What about you? Did you decide to do this overnight? And if not, seems like *you* should have said something." I wasn't upset, just confused.

The plane leveled out, and my stomach dropped again. What was going on in my world?

waiting for it

One corner of Chase's mouth tugged up in a half-grin. "I did. I've been flirting with you for years."

"You talk like that with everyone." It was true. No shame. Last week he practically wrote a soliloquy about how nice Grayson's ass was. "I mean something obvious." Apparently, I was a little dim when it came to the men around me and how they felt about me.

He glided his fingers down my arm, leaving goosebumps in his wake. "You're my sister's best friend. I thought it might be awkward."

"Except, no one cares about that but you."

"No?" He was studying me again with that penetrating gaze that wanted to burrow into my soul. "That hasn't colored the way you see me at all?"

Beyond the thoughts of, *he sees me as a sister and he'd never look at me otherwise*? I shrugged. "No." My denial was less than convincing.

He loosely gripped my fingers and ran his thumb along the back of my knuckle. A million tiny shocks of desire raced through me, and my mouth was suddenly dry. We got drink service on this flight, didn't we? Why was I even thinking about that *now*?

Because my brain was bottlenecked on the *Chase Hughes just kissed me* thing.

"I've been thinking about it for months," Chase said. "Rather, I've been thinking—daydreaming, fantasizing—about you for years. But I didn't know how to bring it up. We have the same friends. If things get awkward between us…"

Our friends would take sides. I didn't want that. But his assumption meant—"You expect things to not work out?" Were we breaking up? We weren't even dating. How did we go from *I'm interested* to *don't make our friends choose between us*? I was over-thinking things.

"I didn't say that." Chase's calm tone was in stark defiance of my racing brain. He let out a light laugh. "You're adorable. You know?"

"What?" Should I be offended? Complimented?

"My money says, right at this very moment, you're starting to run variables through your head. As many as you can grasp. What I mean. What all of this means. What happens next. It's one of the many things I adore about you."

Complimented, I suppose? "Why now?" I still wanted that answer.

"Can I get either of you a drink?" The stewardess interrupted.

Whatever kind of juice they had on hand and vodka. A lot of it. Too bad I had to be in the office in a few hours. "Coke."

waiting for it

"Cup of ice." Chase's gaze never left my face.

The stewardess handed us ice, and me a soda. I pressed the cool can to my face. It didn't sap the heat away the way I hoped.

"I'm kind of glad you and Luke didn't do more than *just kiss.*" Chase was calm. Collected. "In addition to the whole *because I want you* thing. If you'd slept with him, you might not want anyone else. Like me."

—the hell did that come from? "I can draw a lot of assumptions from a statement like that, but my brain is already overloaded. Fill in the blanks for me."

"He and I ran into each other at a bar a few months ago. We talked. We drank. We ended up in bed together." Chase picked up an ice cube and dropped it again.

Fuck my imagination. Now I had a whole new wave of images to tease me. I knew they were both bisexual, but picturing them together… I should be jealous, shouldn't I? Hard to tell, with the want racing through my veins. "Not your best story, but better than one that ends with a bad pun."

"Ah, no. This story had a happy ending. Or a few. At least that night. The sex was great. He's an attentive lover." Chase traced a cold finger along my bottom lip. "I can compete, but you might not have given me a chance if you already knew what he had to offer."

How was I supposed to respond to that? "If he's so incredible, why was it only one night?"

"I couldn't stop thinking about you."

I gently pulled back from his touch. His words, his gaze, and his skin against mine sent a warm, fuzzy glow through me. They also made it hard to think, and there was more to his words than I saw on the surface. There had to be.

"Do you have that problem with every person you hook up with?" I asked.

"Yes. But I have an idea of how you feel about Luke—I've never missed the way you two interact—so it was stronger with him. Besides, I don't do a lot of *hooking up*."

"But the flirting?" I discussed my sex-life details with my girlfriends, but Chase and I weren't *that* close. I'd always assumed...

"Serious with you. Playful with our friends. There's no other flirting."

But... The gears in my brain snagged. Chase was friendly with everyone.

Not the same as flirting.

Maybe not. I'd convinced myself that he treated me like anyone else. Ever since I dated Shawn, and he'd convinced me everything I did was

waiting for it

wrong, I'd had so much trouble trusting my gut, and I didn't dare make that mistake with Chase.

"My point is"—his voice was soft—"you and I are amazing together anyway. If you're interested in more, I'm here."

I was. Definitely. Totally. Mostly.

Why was I hesitating?

Because if we pursued this, it could ruin our friendship. And my friendship with Sadie. And anything I might have with Luke. There was no reward without risk. If things didn't work out with Chase, were we close enough we could recover? Besides, I didn't have anything with Luke. Not like that.

I might if we hadn't been interrupted.

So I'd test the waters with Chase. Not that I was dating Luke. It wasn't even an option. And with Chase... he was right that we had so many friends in common, I'd lose more than just him.

"I need to think about it," I said. More than I already had.

"Will you let me help you decide?"

I should tell him *no*, but curiosity won out. "How?"

"May I kiss you again?"

My heart swooned that he asked permission, and the way he searched my face sent goosebumps speeding up my arms.

"Yes," I said.

He slid his hand to the back of my head and gripped my hair enough to pull, drawing a gasp. He dipped his head, bit my bottom lip, and licked away the sting before crushing his mouth to mine.

Every inch of my body sang in response. I needed something to hold onto, and the only thing I could find was his shirt. I fisted the fabric, terrified if I let go, this would evaporate.

Chase tugged my hair harder, exposing my neck. He kissed along my jaw and up to my earlobe, to nibble.

"I know why you're hesitating," he murmured against the hollow behind my ear.

"Why?" I moaned as much as spoke.

He pulled back to look me in the eye, never letting go. "You're thinking about him. You don't want to let go of what almost was. At the same time, you can see the rift that would run through our group if..." He frowned. "But we'll be incredible together, you and I."

The hint of possession in his voice should turn me off, but it sucked me in deeper.

What would Sadie do?

Not make out with her own brother.

A giggle tried to force its way up, and I swallowed it. *If she wanted it, she'd tell him* yes. "Prove it," I said.

waiting for it

He let go of my hair to trace a finger along the shell of my ear, never dropping my gaze. Intensity simmered between us. When he kissed me again, it was gentler but just as enticing. "Challenge accepted," he said.

My pulse roared in my ears. What had I gotten myself into?

Chapter Seven

Chase plucked an ice cube from his cup and glided it over my heated, swollen lips. He drew a line down my neck and followed the wet trail with another of kisses.

"I have a head full of things I'd love to do to you," he whispered. "And I'm going to see how much of it I can get away with here." He popped the ice in his mouth and kissed me. Ice and heat shocked through me. I whimpered and leaned into the kiss, dancing my tongue around his and the rapidly melting ice.

Chase slipped his hand under my shirt and teased cold fingers up my stomach.

Anticipation, fear, and desire mingled in my veins and pulsed between my legs. Why couldn't I be a wears-skirts kind of person? I leaned in more, and rested my hand on his thigh for balance.

He groaned against my mouth.

When I stroked my fingers over the topography, his groan increased in volume.

waiting for it

I should pull away, but instead I slid higher, stroking his erection through his trousers. Cupping and teasing in response to his grunts and moans.

He worked his fingers under the bottom of my bra. The chill was fading, but not so much I didn't feel the cool when he dragged a thumb over my nipple.

I had to be as wet as his cup of half-melted ice. I continued to tease Chase's shaft and tried not to squirm too much.

"Excuse me." A polite voice interrupted.

I broke away, my face as flaming hot as the rest of my body, to find the stewardess watching us.

"We've had a complaint." Her tone was kind and soft. "Could the two of you"—she gestured—"be less obvious? More discreet?"

"Of course." Chase never missed a beat.

I wanted to sink into my seat and disappear, as the woman strolled away. My desire had intensified, though. Was someone else watching us? What if another passenger was getting off to what we were doing?

Hot.

Fantasy was one thing, but public displays of lewdness got people arrested.

I couldn't look at Chase. "I'm going to read," I mumbled. I lowered my tray table to rest my arms on, so they wouldn't shake, and stared blankly at my phone.

I didn't process a single word in front of me.

"I meant everything I said," Chase murmured.

"So did I." Including the uncertainty.

Silence settled between us again. I should be reading. Or overanalyzing what happened. Instead, I was thinking about Chase's hands, roaming my body.

And Luke. What if he'd been the one to catch us? Would he have watched? Gotten off?

I squeezed my legs together as tightly as I could, but the action didn't do anything to sate my need.

Chase rested a hand on my thigh, under the table. "You're not really reading."

I shook my head. Did the fact that the screen had gone to sleep give me away?

"Keep pretending," he said softly.

What?

He undid my jeans.

I could barely hear over the roar of my heartbeat.

He dipped his fingers under the waistband of my pants. I had to slide down in my seat, to give him better access, and it was still a tight fit.

waiting for it

But Chase's fingers were long and slender, making it easier for him to glide them under my panties.

I was so turned on, when he neared my clit I arched into his touch. I glanced sideways, to find him watching me again. Still? Everything we were doing was hidden by my tray table.

He teased over my clit, sending a shudder through me with each pass. When he focused his attention on the swollen button, I dug my fingers into his arm, needing something to hold onto.

He stroked and circled and nudged me toward orgasm. I bit the inside of my cheek when I came, my ass rising out of my seat.

I dropped back with a breathless gasp, as Chase pulled away.

He sucked his fingers clean, one at a time.

God, this was hot. Had anyone seen us? I risked a glance around. As far as I could tell, no one was paying attention.

"Peaches. My favorite," Chase said.

Luke made a similar comment the other night. Was pussy tasting like peaches some sort of guy-thing I wasn't familiar with?

Getting away with getting off sent boldness through me. "When do I get to return the favor?" I asked. Terror mingled with the hope that he'd ask me to pay him back now.

"There's no favor to return." He was genuine. "This isn't tit for tat. I just wanted to see you come."

"Verdict?"

"Better than any fantasy." He smirked and tangled his fingers with mine.

My brain was going to be a chaotic wreck from here to eternity if he kept this up.

Chapter Eight

I was still processing, as the plane taxied up to the gate and stopped. Chase. And me. It didn't seem real, and at the same time, it was more vivid than anything. Partly because of the pleasant tingle that lingered on my lips. My fingers were intertwined with his and resting on the arm between us. Two hours ago, he was one of the gang. The sexiest one. The only one I fantasized about. But still, nothing more.

And now we were… dating? *Seeing where things go.*

The brush of his lips over my cheek was terrifyingly tender and sweet. "I'm at the vendor's site all day. Text me when you know your plans for tonight, and I'll squeeze myself in," he said.

"All right." There was a good chance he'd have been part of my plans anyway, but this was different. The night might not end with us parting ways at our hotel.

We were among the first to disembark, since we were at the front of the plane, and every few seconds, Chase brushed against me. I was a live wire of nerve endings by the time we reached the gate.

Luke appeared a few minutes later, his gaze flicking between us, one eyebrow raised as he joined us. "How was your flight?" His tone was casual. Same as always.

My cheeks were red, weren't they? Bright, tomato-colored... Now that Chase had reminded me I wore certain emotions on my face, I couldn't stop thinking about it. I started walking toward baggage claim, more to avoid their stares than anything.

Luke joined me, and Chase managed to wedge himself between us, to be by my side.

"Same as yours, but with better amenities." Chase squeezed my hand.

Did Luke see that? Would he know? Did it matter? If Chase and I made this all official and long term, Luke was going to find out anyway.

He and Chase really...? My mind was on other things on the flight, but now, with it flitting back and forth between the two men, I was imagining them together. With me. Without me.

"What about you, Anne?" Luke asked. "Good flight?"

Incredible. Hot. *You should have seen us.* There was so much possibility in that response. "It was good. The extra leg room was nice."

waiting for it

"Hmm. Cool." Luke wandered toward a newspaper- and gift-shop, and we drifted that way with him. He didn't dwell, instead falling into step on my other side and brushing his arm against mine.

Was that on purpose? Had he always made casual contact with me when we walked side-by-side? No. I would have noticed.

Then again, I'd convinced myself for years that neither of them was flirting with me. That Chase wasn't interested. That Luke was just extra friendly.

"Rumor is some couple up in Business Class was practically fucking each other. Did you see them?" Luke's question was calm. Casual.

If I'd been drinking, I would have choked. I could picture it in my head.

Chase traced his fingers over the back of my knuckles. "*Practically fucking* isn't accurate at all."

My body was on fire, and so was my face, but for very different reasons. I needed to find the closest hole to climb in and hide.

"Hmm..." Luke was saying a lot of that today. "I hope the show was good."

Chase chuckled. "You like a good show?"

"All depends on who the stars are."

"You would have loved this one," Chase said.

Forget the hole. I needed to yank both of them into a corner and do something hot enough to land us on a porn site. Embarrassment was fading, replaced with that rush I felt when the stewardess asked us to stop. The potential of both humiliation and someone else getting off to the sight of the three of us together lingered on my tongue. I could feel Luke's hands gliding up my chest, his lips on my neck. All while Chase worked his fingers lower, sucked on my throat—

"Annie?" Chase's tone implied I'd missed something.

I shook the fantasy aside. It was hard to walk and clench my thighs together at the same time, anyway. "Sorry—what?"

"Sushi tonight? Chase knows a fantastic place." If Luke was asking, was he going to invite everyone in the office?

I was turned on by the idea of an audience, but that was different than dinner with co-workers I barely knew outside of video conferences. "Work?" Wow, that came out dumb. "I mean, I'm not sure I know how to deal with a night off."

Luke tickled his fingers lightly along my arm. "I'm ordering you to take tonight off, as your boss, and the three of us will go explore the city for a few hours."

Yes, sir. The sassy retort froze on my lips. "Yes, sir." Maybe I shouldn't have said that out loud. Too late to take it back.

waiting for it

We reached the carousel for our bags, and Chase slid an arm around my waist.

The gesture was warm. Comforting. Possessive. Was I okay with that?

"I didn't realize the two of you were more than friends." Luke's tone was impossible to read. Then again, I'd been misreading it for a long time.

"We weren't. Were?" And now I couldn't speak. Did Luke think I'd been making out with him even though I was with someone else? "Just friends. We were just friends before."

"We had a *conversation* on the plane." Chase's emphasis was distinct.

"Hmm."

I was starting to really dislike Luke's non-committal grunt. Mostly because I couldn't interpret it.

"Did it go better than the *conversation* you and I had?" Luke asked

Chase squeezed my hip. "She gave me permission to try to win her over."

"Then I want the same." There wasn't much room for misinterpretation in Luke's words this time.

That didn't stop me from asking, "What?"

Luke stepped in front of me and held my gaze. "I want permission to try to win you over."

Were they really almost-fighting over me? This wasn't happening. There was no way. I held up my arm and pinched. *Ow.*

"Anne?" Luke raised an eyebrow.

Chase dipped his head near my ear. "It's not a dream. I promise." The heat of his stage whisper danced over my skin.

"Dream-you would say that." I refused to be stunned silent, even as I struggled to process what was going on.

"There's a dream version of me?" Chase trailed his nose along the shell of my ear. "What else does he say? Would you like me to provide him with some explicit dialog for his next appearance?"

This was over the top. I loved the idea and the attention, but it was too much. Straight out of some imitation of an *Alpha hero always gets what he wants* romance novel. "You're both yanking my chain." That had to be it. *Including those kisses?* "There are hidden cameras?" *The kind that land us on Smut Central?* My brain needed to stop. "Will I see this on YouTube in the morning and have to pray it doesn't go viral?"

Chase spun me to face him, and cupped my cheeks between his hands. A whimper stuck in my throat at the intensity in his gaze and touch.

waiting for it

"I would *never* do that to you." He sounded hurt, but he wasn't as sparkling good and innocent as that tone implied.

"You told Sadie that Jax called her names, and you did it to keep them apart."

Chase dropped his hands, tilted his head back, and let out a frustrated groan, before looking at me again. "Ten years ago. *Fuck.* We all made mistakes in high school. I thought we were over that."

Luke grasped my hand, drawing my attention, and rested a finger under my chin.

I was learning to like that as much as I disliked his generic *hmm*.

"I don't know what he's up to, but I'm not willing to let you go that easily unless you tell me to leave you alone," he said. "The only thing holding me back was I don't want you to think—"

"That my job is on the line. I get it." That was the one thing I *did* understand. But this appeared to be exactly what the two of them said it was—these gorgeous men were fighting over me.

A barking laugh escaped my throat.

Chase and Luke stared at me, questioning expressions on their handsome faces.

"Care to share the joke?" Chase asked.

That was what I wanted to say to them. This was happening—except shit like this didn't happen in the actual world.

"Um… Okay. You can both try to win me over." It felt ludicrous, saying the words, but at the same time, I was looking forward to the ride.

"Good." Chase grinned. Gripping my hips, he pulled me back to him and crushed his mouth to mine.

A fresh wave of desire spilled through me. *God*, I loved everything about his kisses. How was this my life now?

Chapter Nine

My lips were still tingling when Chase stepped off the shuttle for his car-rental company.

"Looks like I need to up my game." Luke sounded more entertained than put out.

I fell into step beside him as we headed for our car. "Please don't."

"I don't understand."

"I can only handle so much smoldering intensity." I kept the teasing in my reply. We reached the car, and I set my bags on the ground.

Instead of opening the trunk, Luke turned to me. "And you're getting your fill from Chase?" Amusement overrode the hurt in his voice. He stepped toward me, and I backed up until I collided with a cement pillar. "You don't want to be pressed against the wall?" Luke grabbed my wrists in a single swoop and pinned them over my head. His body molded to mine. "Devoured, until your legs are weak and your voice is hoarse?" he growled against my skin.

I didn't fight my whimper. "I never said that."

"You sure?" Luke let go and put some distance between us.

Did. Not. Like. I wanted his body fitted against mine again. "I just don't want to lose the fun." I could do this. Handle the flirting and be normal around him. I'd been psyching myself up to do that for more than a day now. It came more easily than I thought. "All I'm saying is, give me as much Ryan Reynolds as Gomez Adams."

"So… masturbating with a unicorn?" Luke winked before turning away to load our things into the back of the car.

"I could get into it if that's your thing."

"I don't come in rainbows."

I laughed at the visual and his playful retort. "Probably good."

"Happy to prove it."

My brain stalled, but only for a heartbeat this time. I could do this. "Even better. Do you think if you ate a handful of Skittles first, I could taste the rainbow?"

He sucked a sharp breath through his teeth and shook his head. "The things you do to my imagination…"

Me? To him?

"We should get going." Luke opened the passenger door for me. "Otherwise, we may not make it to the office."

waiting for it

Responsibility warred with desire, as I slid into the car. "Office. Right."

We left airport parking and were pulling onto the freeway, when Luke's phone rang. Just a few minutes earlier, and I'd think the damn thing was trying to interrupt us.

He pulled it from his pocket and handed it to me. "Anyone important?"

"Scott." My gut sank. Did the company CTO regularly make casual calls to Luke? "Answering. Putting on speaker." I swiped as I talked.

"Hello." Luke spoke loudly and clearly.

"How far out are you?" Scott was usually friendly. Chatty. The way he cut straight to the point was less than reassuring.

His abrupt tone kicked my stomach into my shoes. "Just left the airport," I said.

"Good. You're both there. Something came out of Sacramento today." Scott let out a long sigh. "Someone published the entire game plot, including our surprise ending, online."

"What? Why?" I knew why, but it was easier to ask than admit someone with access to that information—someone so close to this project— was trying to fuck us.

"Next steps." Luke had lost any hint of playfulness and was all business.

Hot.

"Chloe's already released five other variations in the same forums, to confuse things. Yoshi is handling everything else public-facing," Scott said. "Zane emailed you machine information. I need you to find out who this came from and deal with them."

"On it. We'll check in soon," Luke said.

Dread hung heavy in my limbs as we disconnected from Scott. As if missed deadlines weren't enough, now we were dealing with sabotage—espionage?—too. "Nice of someone to set up a welcome present for us." My sarcasm came out with more bitterness and less teasing than I intended.

"Yay." Luke scrubbed a hand through his short hair. "When we get in, Mike and I are going to talk. I need you chatting with developers. Keep it informal. Fast. Don't plan on getting a lot of your own coding done today."

"Right." I hated the idea of losing a day of work, but this was important too.

Luke rested a hand on my knee. The shock of heat was muffled by stress. "I'm glad you're here." He gently squeezed my leg. "No one else I trust more to get us through this."

It wasn't filthy or sexy, but it did summon a ball of warmth in my chest that spread through me.

We spent the rest of the drive modifying our plans for the week. I watched the scenery pass by in

waiting for it

a hazy blur. I'd taken several trips out here, and always loved the scenery. Today, I couldn't see a lot of it.

Wildfires were tearing through the hills, not too far away, and the air was choked with smoke. We had summer fires in Salt Lake, but nothing this severe. I hated that so many of our programmers were dealing with the evacuation and the fear of losing their homes on top of a deadline and a visit from the boss.

We arrived at the building and headed straight for the floor where the developers worked. My first few times here, doing this felt awkward. Like walking into a stranger's home and making myself comfortable. But now, it was almost as familiar as walking into my own office.

The location Luke, Chase, and I worked in was Rinslet's international headquarters. Rinslet didn't have the same kind of massive campus that some of the bigger tech companies had, but they owned the entire building downtown, and it was one of the taller ones in the city. There was a little of everything on-site—cafeteria, gym, gaming room.

This was a satellite location for developers, so we only took up a floor. Everyone in the open-floor plan had their heads down and fingers flying over keys when we stepped into the room. A few people looked up, and then several more, and whispers fluttered through the air.

Luke growled softly. "Mike was supposed to let them know," he muttered.

"He's as busy as the rest of us." My defense came instinctively. I preferred to think the best of most people, but in Mike's case, I wasn't so sure that was wise.

"Hey, guys." Speak of the devil. Mike strode from his office, meeting us halfway. "I hope your flight was good. Glad you're here. Conference Room Gamma is set up for you to work in. You speak to Scott yet?"

Luke nodded. "You and I need to talk." He glanced at me. "You good?"

"Yeah." I was in my element here. There shouldn't be any hidden surprises, like my boss and my best friend's brother agreeing to compete for my affection.

I headed for the conference room and set up my laptop. I was getting ready to talk to the first person on my schedule, when my phone buzzed with a group text from Sadie and Lyn.

How was your flight? Sadie asked.

Shit, I forgot to text them when I landed. And I needed to tell them what had me distracted, too. How was I going explain this to Sadie?

Chapter Ten

I'm here. I'm good. Sorry about the delay. I sent the message.

In my mind, I added, *I would have replied sooner, but I was lost in the afterglow of your brother fingering me on the plane.* That wasn't going to work so great. It wasn't as though I intended to keep what was going on with Chase a secret, but Sadie, Lyn, and I shared all sorts of details about our love lives, and this one wasn't going to be so simple to dive into.

Did Chase already tell her? Probably not, but it was possible.

As long as you're all right, Lyn wrote.

Was I? I was a little confused, but the adrenaline racing through my veins, and the way my pulse whimpered every time I thought about either man, said I was pretty fucking good. *I am. And as soon as I get home, I have to tell you both something.* What if Chase *did* tell Sadie first? *It's a good thing, and I'm not keeping it a secret, so if you hear anything before then, just remember this is a story told better face-to-face.*

Yeah, I was that friend who typed the mile-long single text messages.

That's not fair, Lyn said.

Sadie's reply was only a second behind. *Especially with a lead-in like that.*

True. Hearing I had to wait for more info would drive me nuts, but I had to look Sadie in the eye when I told her. *I know.*

When are you free? Sadie asked.

No clue. Today is going to be nuts.

Facetime us, Lyn said. *First thing in the morning tomorrow. We'll be waiting.*

Sounds fair. TTYL

The rest of my day could go that smoothly, and I wouldn't complain.

I dove into work.

A few minutes later, Luke joined me.

There wasn't much conversation. Deadlines called, and we both had a long to-do list that had grown even more with this morning's security breach.

Time ticked away, punctuated by the clack of fingers flying over keyboards.

Was Luke staring at me? I looked up to meet his gaze.

waiting for it

"You're adorable when you're focused. Have you ever noticed?" He asked.

How was I supposed to reply to that? The attention was amazing, but it also felt almost like too much. "Have I ever noticed how I look when I'm working? Can't say I have."

"I'm pouring on too much, aren't I?" He scrubbed his face. "It's been killing me, to keep my distance."

I should be concentrating on my work, but I couldn't turn away from this. "Why now? Not-that-I-mind." I swallowed, trying to gather my thoughts. "But, why now?"

"That kiss the other night undid me. Everything was right in that room."

"Including the broken code?"

Luke's smirk was worth the joke. "Maybe not that part. But when I saw you with Chase in the airport, I had to say something. This can't be a total surprise. I've never completely held back."

Yeah, but thanks to my past, I didn't trust the little voice in my head telling me, *he's flirting*. I still didn't completely trust it. I shouldn't be bothered that Luke was laying the attention on so heavily, if I needed a flashing beacon to get me to listen. Then again, I'd seen such bold affection mean bad things in the past. "I wasn't sure."

"And now?"

I still wasn't sure. How fucked up was that? "I'm looking forward to the discovery stage." And I wanted to change the subject. If I lingered on Luke while I was in the middle of overthinking him, I'd say things I couldn't take back. "We need to shift the QA schedule on the Groundrim final boss. We have before Sloth City, but the components won't be ready first." Work-talk—my trusty conversation fallback.

"Where are you looking?" Luke pushed back from his laptop and came around to stand behind me.

"Here." I pointed at the project timeline and forced myself to ignore how close he stood. That with the dip of his head, he could kiss my neck.

"Hmm." He leaned in, resting his hands on the table and bracketing my arms. "Make the change. Let Ben know." Ben was our project manager.

"Will do." I waited for Luke to pull away.

He didn't.

Did he expect me to work while he watched?

"I wish I'd been there on the plane." Luke's voice shifted, taking on a low, gravelly vibe.

Not what I was expecting. "So you could have stopped us?"

"No." He snorted. "I would have helped."

waiting for it

My mind blanked. Coated in a bucket of white, there was nothing there. "You're not jealous?" Was I missing something about this *competition*?

He rested his head against the back of my mine. "I would have watched. I would have helped." His words hummed through and around me. "If there was a lock on the conference-room door, I'd bend you over the table right now, and find out if you're as tight as I imagine."

God, there was no way I could ignore the desire spilling through me. Could we wedge a chair under the door handle? "And now we'll never get any work done again." It wasn't the most awkward thing I could have said, but it made the list.

"Sure we will. Same way we always have."

"You've got a lot more faith in us than I do," I teased. I needed this conversation to take a lighter turn.

"I've got absolute faith in you." Luke still had that deep, soul-seducing tone as he pulled away and returned to his seat.

I was wrong to think Chase was the intense one. Luke was going to consume me from the inside out.

Someone knocked on the conference room door, and Mike stepped into the room. "Do you guys have a minute?"

Sure. As soon as I dislodged my heart from my stomach. What if he'd done that two minutes earlier? Did I look guilty?

"What's up?" Luke sounded much calmer than I felt. I needed to learn that trick.

Mike pulled up a chair at the far end of the conference table. "We just got an email." He looked at me. "Are you all right? You look flushed."

Fuck. "I'm fine." I gave him a weak smile. "Long night. Distracted today. Email from whom?"

"Zane. Says he tracked down where the original upload came from. It was one of our remote build machines."

Zane was head of cyber security. The fact that he was handling this personally, rather than giving it to someone on his team, was another reminder of how critical the event was. I shoved the flirting from a moment earlier into a box, and opened my email. There wasn't much more information there than Mike provided. "So we still don't have anything."

"We do." Mike winced. "We have several other indicators that point to Billie. Logins. Change management."

That didn't seem right. "Zane doesn't mention those."

"We've been... uh... lax with security." The hesitation in Mike's tone hung heavy in the room.

waiting for it

"With the tight deadlines. The crunch. Some things slip."

Nope. Still didn't buy it. His story had holes.

"You're sharing login information?" Luke sounded as skeptical as I felt.

Mike shook his head like a bobble in an earthquake. "No. Of course not. Not passwords or anything. But someone is on the machine, and they let another dev hop on to look at shared work. And Billie… She's been off lately." He looked at Luke. "Hitting on a couple of the guys. Making everyone uncomfortable with certain jokes."

Mike's biggest excuse seemed to be *we don't like following protocol*, and if that bit everyone in the ass, I was going to be pissed. But his story felt more *off* the longer he talked. I knew Billie. She'd been with the company for a couple of years, and she was top notch. She was also reserved and mostly kept to herself. I had a hard time seeing her as being on the giving end of sexual harassment, intentional or not.

But if Mike felt uncomfortable with her, was it my place to judge? "You talked to HR?" I asked.

He never looked at me. "It's not a big deal. But if she's taking things too far…"

"Why would she go from dirty jokes to corporate sabotage?" I was missing something.

He kept his attention on Luke. "*You* wanted information about the situation here. I'm providing it."

"Answer Anne's question," Luke said.

I appreciated the support, but not that it had to be offered. If my face was red now, it was thanks to the irritation flickering inside.

Mike rolled his eyes. "I don't know why Billie would fuck us all out of our jobs because we didn't like a few of her pussy jokes. Maybe you should ask her."

"You're the one making the suppositions. I'm asking you." I let anger slide into my tone.

"And I gave you an answer. What are you pissed about?"

Being ignored. Talked down to. Hearing another female programmer take the blame out of the gate. Was I in the wrong?

The moment the question popped into my head, I wanted to flatten it with a mallet, but it was here now and it wasn't leaving. Would I have put up the same kind of opposition if he'd been talking about one of the guys on the team? Did that make me the bad guy?

"That's all I needed to know." I kept the self-doubt out of my retort and stared at my screen, trying to force my brain to stop sabotaging me.

waiting for it

"Thanks for the info. Keep us both posted," Luke said. "Wait," he added, when Mike reached for the door. "Anne's right to ask."

"Of course she is." Mike left.

I liked that Luke had my back, but now that I was questioning things, his support got tacked onto the list. Why wouldn't he take my side? He was trying to fuck me.

He would have backed me up anyway.

But he's been watching me a lot longer than I realized. Because I'm shit at reading a situation.

Not true.

Isn't it?

Best thing to do when my mind was plotting to undo me like this was focus on coding. Something I tended to get right, because I could follow a list of rules and not have to interpret anything. No more people decisions for me.

Chapter Eleven

My nagging brain plus an early morning flight plus no sleep last night sank into my bones. As the clock drew closer to five, I felt like I'd been compressed to preserve bandwidth, and parsed incorrectly on the other side.

The fun with Chase and Luke this morning felt like someone else's life.

My phone buzzed at the same time as Luke's chimed, and we executed a perfect ballet of reaching for the devices. It was a group text from Chase.

Would you rather stay in?

I'd drop a lot for their company, either of them, even before this, but I wasn't up for exploring the city. If I turned him down, would the fun end?

"I'm not going to answer on your behalf, but I also won't be offended if you tell him *yes,*" Luke said.

"What about sushi?" I spoke the words aloud as I typed them. Was that silly? Luke would read

waiting for it

my reply, but he was also sitting in the room with me.

Chase replied seconds later. *They deliver. Besides, you've had a long few days, and my money says you don't want to go out. I don't care where we are, as long as I have your company.*

That was sweet. Almost cheesy, but in a way that warmed me from the inside out. *Okay. Let's stay in.*

Meet you both at the hotel, Chase wrote.

Luke and I finished work with minimal conversation. The pauses were comfortable, like what I was used to, as long as I didn't think too much about the night ahead. Every time I started down that path, I ran into so many questions, my brain stalled. Did they really expect me to choose between them? So far, it didn't feel like it. How did this work tonight? I was used to dinner with either of them, but together as more than friends…? What was I supposed to tell Sadie and Lyn in the morning? Was this a good idea?

I had to shake it all aside, or I'd freeze up from indecision and doubt. Or worse, I'd pick an answer to each question, and it would be the wrong one.

Chase wasn't at the hotel yet, but we needed to check in anyway. There was only one person behind the counter, so Luke let me go first.

I gave the desk clerk a friendly smile and my name.

She typed. And then some more. A line creased her forehead. "I'm sorry—can you spell your last name for me again?"

"Fortier. F. O. R. T. I. E. R. And it's *Anne* with an *e*."

"Like the show?" She smiled.

"Exactly."

She typed a bit more. "I'm sorry. I don't see a reservation for you."

No big deal. My name wasn't in there quite right or something. "Maybe *Anne* without an *e*? Or my last name is wrong?"

She shook her head. "We don't have reservations for any *Annes* tonight. Regardless of spelling."

"Is there an issue?" Luke joined me.

"She can't find my reservation." I wasn't near panic, but I was getting concerned.

He frowned. "Look under *Luke Rider*."

The desk clerk worried her bottom lip. "You're not in here either."

"We are. My assistant made the reservations yesterday." Luke grabbed his phone, jabbed the screen a few times, and showed it to her. "Here's the confirmation email from our travel agency."

waiting for it

She looked between phone and computer, typing some more. Clicking. "I'm sorry. That information isn't in here. And we don't have any available rooms. We're full up because of evacuations and such. I'm sorry."

Luke clenched his jaw, and tension ran through his frame. When he looked like this, he was almost scary. A starkly abrupt reminder of the Marine past he never talked about.

He stepped away with a glance at me. "Let me make some calls."

The travel agency was closed for the day, so we split up the list of nearby hotels and started making calls. I got the same answer with my first three, and it didn't sound like Luke's luck was any better.

Chase arrived, and his smile when his gaze met mine chased away the stress.

"What's going on?"

Luke's groan of frustration echoed around us.

I gave Chase a brief rundown of our lack of accommodations.

He held up his index finger. "Don't go anywhere." He approached the desk and exchanged words, ID, and a credit card with the woman who hadn't been able to help us. Her frown vanished by the end of the conversation.

I understood how she felt.

Chase joined us again and handed us each a keycard.

"Must be nice to have all those frequent-traveler points." Luke's tone was light, with the slightest twinge.

Chase gave him a dry smile. "Not as nice as you're assuming. They still don't have any extra rooms, but I have double queen beds, and the couch pulls out, so all three of us can share a room. If you're interested."

"I'm in." My reply slipped out without thought. I'd spent a large portion of my teenage years sleeping at Sadie and Chase's. Luke's raised eyebrow made me wish I could take the words back.

"Me too." Luke shrugged. "I'm not missing out again if anything happens."

"Sleepover." I tried to toss the word out with careless abandon, and not think about whether it sounded silly or not. And I definitely wasn't thinking about the implications of Luke's reply.

Just kidding. I totally was.

"I don't have enough hair to style, but I'll rock the flimsy teddy," Luke said. "This includes giggly pillow fights, right?"

Chase rolled his eyes. "That's not how a sleepover works. We're going to need a lot of pizza and to expect not to sleep."

waiting for it

"That's not a sleepover; that's my life." The teasing made it easier to ignore my trepidation about what this might become. These were the same two men I always laughed and joked with. Just because they'd shifted our relationships in the last few days... "Besides, I was promised sushi."

Luke bowed deeply. "And sushi you shall have, m'lady."

Chase grabbed my bags before I could, and we headed upstairs.

The room was one of those business suites with a separate bedroom and a reasonably sized living room.

Luke tossed his bag near the sofa as soon as we walked in the room. "I'll take the couch."

"That doesn't seem fair. Shouldn't we draw straws or something?" While I had no idea what to expect from tonight, it was nice to know he hadn't just assumed we'd end up in bed together. Sweet, even.

Chase opened his mouth.

"Nope." Luke cut him off. "It's Chase's room, that he was kind enough to share, and neither of us is letting you sleep on the couch, Anne."

"That's true. I was going to say that. He just beat me to it," Chase said.

It still didn't feel right. "Am I allowed to argue this logic?"

They both shook their heads, and Chase put my bags in the bedroom. "Ordering the sushi," he called. "Tell me if there's anything you won't eat."

"Pretty sure everyone here's fine with any sort of meat," Luke said.

That was true, whether he was talking food or sexual preference, and the way things were going today, I assumed both were legitimate topics.

We made small talk and caught up on each other's days, while we waited for food to arrive. No one sat next to anyone, which felt odd. But cramming three people onto the couch so we could all be together, or any combination of pairing off also seemed weird.

How was this supposed to work?

Dinner was more of the same. When we were done, we drifted into the bedroom, to watch TV *someplace more comfortable*, but that left the awkward question of who was supposed to sit where.

I'd never dated two guys at once before, especially not at the exact same moment. Was this a date? Was this three friends hanging out?

"Three people in one tiny space, sharing a single bathroom. Just like college." Chase's comment was a welcome distraction from my questions.

waiting for it

Luke raised an eyebrow. "Including the sexual experimentation?"

"I'd pretty much moved onto the *doing* rather than *experimenting* by then," Chase said.

"I'm more of a late bloomer." I let the reply roll casually off my tongue. It wasn't a secret in our inner circle that I was bi, but I dated mostly men, so sometimes claiming anything other than *straight* felt like I was an impostor. "I never even thought about it until Shawn." It didn't matter how much time had passed. His name was rancid on my tongue.

Chase's distorted expression mirrored my bitterness. I didn't want to ruin the evening with bad memories. Why did I bring up my ex?

"Who's Shawn?" Luke looked between us.

Chase mimicked spitting. "A fucking asshole."

That's what everyone said back then, too. I wished I'd listened to my friends, rather than the boyfriend who ran my ego into the ground. "A guy I went out with." I didn't want to leave Luke hanging, but I wasn't going to linger on details. How little information would let us move back to more fun topics? "He used to tease me about the kind of porn I like. Would ask me all the time if I was a secret lesbian who was going to leave him for a woman. After he and I broke up, I started talking about it with…" Another confession. What was up with me spilling so many secrets tonight?

Luke and Chase both leaned in. "With whom?" they asked at the same time.

"A friend. We're talking about experimentation, right? She helped me figure a few things out." There. Conversation was back to neutral. We could have fun again.

Chase frowned. "Wait. Not Sadie. Please say not Sadie."

"Why? Because you still think you can say who your sister hooks up with?" I tried to keep the defensive tone from my voice.

"No. Because then the story isn't spank-bank material."

My cheeks heated to flaming. He was... to me? "It wasn't Sadie. It was Lyn."

Luke whistled. "He's right. Definitely fantasy material."

"That's not fair." My retort slipped out before I could stop it. Why? Because I'd been trying for so long to *not* fantasize about either of them? "You get new visuals, and I don't?"

Chase smirked. "You've got a better imagination. Picture me with whomever you'd like."

"No, she's right. Fair's fair." Luke crushed his mouth to Chase's.

Chapter Twelve

The way Luke kissed Chase wasn't a simple peck on the lips. It was one of those hungry, all-consuming kisses I felt just from watching. The kind where I knew exactly why they were both groaning and breathless.

When they broke apart, Chase growled. "I'm definitely in for that."

"Totally hot and masturbation-worthy." I fanned myself.

Luke turned his attention back to me. "What other fantasies do you have?"

"Well… I have one, but it's risqué. Almost taboo in today's society."

Both guys leaned in closer.

"A full week off work without being called in, and eight hours of sleep on every one of those nights," I said.

Chase licked his bottom lip. "I always suspected you had a filthy, kinky side."

Luke tossed up his hands. "Too much for me. You're way out of my depth."

"What did you have in mind?" I asked with a laugh.

"I'll show you how it starts." Chase grasped my fingertips and tugged me to my feet. He cradled my face. His kiss had the same intensity as those we shared on the plane—soft but insistent and all-consuming. He nibbled my lips. My jaw. My ears and neck. The drawn-out attention sent goosebumps racing over me.

All while Luke watched. If he was enjoying this even half as much as I liked seeing the two of them kiss, that made the whole thing even hotter. It didn't matter that Chase kept his kisses above my shoulders; my entire body was a live wire.

I didn't know how long we stayed pressed together, but when he pulled back he wore a lazy grin. "That's how the fantasy *starts*."

"It's a fair appetizer." Luke stepped forward.

My gaze dropped to his crotch without thought. When I saw the outline of his erection, it took a moment to look up again.

He was smirking. "My fantasies tend to be more direct. We start with the main course."

"Which is?" I was enjoying this game, especially with Luke looking at me like I was dinner.

He pressed his hand to my throat, applying just enough weight to nudge me back against the wall.

waiting for it

He crushed his mouth to mine and his body to mine and devoured my moans and gasps. It was only a kiss, but the way we fit together, the way my body molded to his, the way his hard form teased every inch of me drew me to life. It was intense and terrifying and incredible. Especially when he squeezed his thumb in, making my head light.

I gasped for more when he pulled away. He glanced at Chase. "Do you have a comeback?"

"I'm enjoying the show too much for that."

"*That's* one of my fantasies." It was easier to admit it when someone else said it.

Luke's grin was dangerous. "Being used and fucked for an audience who gets off on your pleasure?"

His phrasing made me tingle everywhere. "Yes."

Luke guided me to the widest space of empty floor between the foot of the beds. The way Chase watched me and Luke still gripped my neck, combined with their lingering kisses on my skin, had an insistent pulse throbbing between my legs.

Luke moved to stand behind me and glided his hands up my sides, under my shirt. His palms were hot and rough. "Arms up."

I complied, and he tugged my shirt over my head. Technically, my bra wasn't any more revealing than a bikini top, which Chase had seen me in more times than I could count, but this felt different. My heart hammered against my ribs.

Luke pushed my jeans to the floor, and like that, I was standing in the middle of a hotel room in nothing but a bra and panties, while two gorgeous guys stared at me.

The lust and desire filling the air were almost tangible. I couldn't remember ever being more aroused.

Luke unsnapped my bra and slid it down my arms. In a move so fluid I barely registered how he did it, he tugged my hands behind my back and had them bound with the lingerie.

He slapped one of my ass cheeks.

I sucked in a sharp breath through my teeth. Not what I expected.

"Is that a good gasp or a bad one?" he asked.

"Definitely good."

Luke alternated sides, slapping one butt cheek then the other, each smack reverberating through the room. The sound was as much a turn-on as the lingering sting.

He glided his hand lightly along the curve of my ass. I was torn between closing my eyes and sinking into the abruptly gentle touch, or watching Chase watch me.

Luke slipped his hand between my legs from behind and pressed into the crotch of my panties,

waiting for it

drawing a new moan. He teased through fabric until I was swaying with his touch. He shoved the cotton aside and slipped two fingers into me without warning. "*Fuck*, baby doll. You're soaked. You like a little filth in your life?"

"Yes." My reply came out timid and breathy. The sensation of having something inside me was delicious.

"Sweet, sweet Anne." He pumped. In and out. In and out. Deeper with each thrust. "I guess it's true what they say—the nerdy ones can be extra dirty."

Could I be? I never had been before—not with anything but what I watched online—but Luke's tone and Chase's gaze made me want to bend to their will. "I'll be whatever you want."

"Mmm... I like the sound of that." Luke withdrew, and I whimpered with disappointment. "What if I want you to beg?"

"Please?" I poured my desperation into the word.

Luke didn't touch me, but his breath caressed my neck. "*Please* what?"

"Please make me come?"

Luke and Chase both groaned.

"Since you asked so sweetly..." Luke slipped his hand between my legs again.

I moaned when he found my clit. I was so wound up, it didn't take much circling and stroking, to draw me to orgasm. Waves of pleasure crashed over me, and I ground into his hand until it was too much and my body jerked away.

Luke pressed into my back, one hand on my stomach, keeping me stable when my legs wobbled underneath me. He shoved his sticky fingers into my mouth. "Tell me how good you taste, baby doll."

"So good." My words were muffled by his fingers. I'd never understood the fascination with this, but right now it was better than candy. I sucked greedily, driven by his groans of encouragement.

Chase stepped up to kiss me. Our tongues mingled with each other and around Luke's fingers. So apparently this *could* get hotter.

"Seems I can only watch for so long," Chase murmured between licks and kisses.

"I'm as happy to have you here as over there," I said.

"I know I said earlier you didn't owe me, and you don't. But since we're talking about fantasies, on the plane—and several other places throughout my life—I was absolutely dreaming of your lips wrapped around my cock." he said.

I stared at Chase with wide eyes and licked my lips. Did that look sultry? I hoped so. "Okay."

waiting for it

"Kneel on the corner of the bed." Luke's tone left no room for argument.

I did, then I crawled toward Chase and, holding his gaze, grabbed his zipper between my teeth and tugged it down.

The gravel in his moan was intoxicating when I kissed along the hard outline in his trousers.

He freed himself, and I flicked my tongue over the head of his cock, before taking him into my mouth.

Looking up at him as he watched me sent a fresh rush of need pulsing through me. I licked and sucked, using his grunts as cues.

When he knotted his fingers in my hair, holding me in place, I gasped. He struck the back of my throat. I bit back the gag and relaxed around his length.

I heard the tear of foil. A condom? A moment later, Luke glided his cock along my slit, startling me and cranking my arousal higher. He slipped up and down a few times, before gliding inside me. "Fuuuuck." He gripped my hips tightly. "I love seeing you like this. Flushed. Wet. Sucking on a thick cock while I'm buried balls deep in your cunt. So fucking sexy."

His crude words were as enticing as any touch and spurred me on. I wanted him to fuck me, fill me up, and whisper filthy things in my ear forever, while he called me *baby doll*. I shouldn't like the nickname, but the way Luke said it, I wanted to be his everything.

I rocked between the two men, falling into a haze of ecstasy. The pace picked up. Luke pounded harder. Chase struck the back of my throat with every thrust, though he had his fist wrapped around the base of his cock.

"*God*, Annie. I'm so close." Chase pulled back, stroking his shaft.

I stared up at him, desire and desperation coursing through me. "Come in my mouth?" I pleaded.

That earned me another pair of grunts that felt like the most delicious praise, and Chase forced himself between my lips again.

A salty spurt hit the back of my throat, and then kept going. The noises Chase made, sharp and punctuated, were a million tiny fingers dancing over my skin.

He knelt to kiss me, licking himself from my lips. He reached a hand between my legs. When he found my clit, my body shuddered away, still tender.

Luke covered Chase's fingers before he could withdraw, and used both their hands to stroke my clit.

Orgasm rushed up fast, tearing a scream from my throat and flooding my entire body. I clenched around the shaft buried inside me. I felt like all of me opened up.

Luke's grunts grew punctuated then stuttered, reaching a frantic pace, before he slowed to a stop. We all sat there, panting. The cool air kissed the sweat from my skin, and Luke trailed his tongue up my spine, doing the same.

"I think you left a wet spot," he muttered.

I'd never done that before. "Sorry."

"Never be sorry for that." Chase was studying me with adoration that made my pulse kick up again.

"I guess we'll have to use the other bed." Most of the growl was gone from Luke's voice, but I still heard the undercut.

My dreams were going to be filled with wet, sticky sex and *baby doll* for a long time.

Chapter Thirteen

We cleaned up and collapsed in the other bed.

I felt more exposed than I was used to. Pinned between Luke and Chase was the perfect way to be. I kind of loved this feeling of being vulnerable but safe with them. Like I could let my guard down here.

And the happy fuzziness in my brain was blocking out most of the *but what now?* questions that had nagged me all day.

"You're not really going to sleep on the couch, are you?" I asked Luke.

"As opposed to…"

If none of us moved, things would be perfect forever. "We could all sleep here. Like this."

"It's a tight fit." Chase squeezed my hip. The gentle gesture felt possessive. And perfect.

"That's what she said." Luke grinned.

I laughed. Nothing had changed, except that we'd all just had the dirtiest sex I'd ever been part of. Just a teensy, tiny, tremendous thing.

waiting for it

Behind me, Chase shifted. "If you both want to stay here, I don't mind. We'll just have to snuggle close."

"Yes, please." That sounded so completely right. Even better than a week of regular sleep.

Luke kissed the tip of my nose. "Is this what you had in mind when you said *sleepover?*"

"It will be going forward. Past sleepovers for me have involved a lot more talking and a lot less fingering." Not counting the experimentation with Lyn.

Chase sighed heavily. "Fantasies dashed."

"What fantasies?" Luke looked past me. "You were in the same house when these things happened, as I understand it."

"Yeah, but that was no man's land," Chase said. "I was *not* allowed in that part of the house when the girls were over."

They'd confessed their long-term attraction. I could do the same. "I never would have minded."

"See? You miss one-hundred percent of the shots you don't take," Luke said.

Chase made a gagging sound. "Did you just motivational-poster us?"

"It *was* kind of creepy." I had to agree. "Can't you say that in a funny voice—maybe Jerry Seinfeld or something—and take the edge off?"

"Out on the edge, you can see all sorts of things you can't see from the center." Luke finished the phrase with a stoic look that was disrupted by his trying not to smirk.

I knew that one. "Vonnegut? You're full of wisdom tonight."

"He's full of something." Every time Chase spoke, his chest hummed against my back.

Luke tucked a strand of hair behind my ear. "Adoration, horniness, and fuck-you-till-you-screamitude."

"You didn't exhaust your supply with the last round?" I was pleasantly sleepy.

"Hmm…" Luke screwed up his face. "Gorgeous woman in my arms, and my naked cock pressed against your bare stomach? Easy supply to replenish."

I smirked at the twitch against my abdomen.

"Wait. You're buying this? I can do motivational quotes too," Chase said.

I only had so much appreciation for that sort of thing, even wrapped up in two men and post-coital bliss. "Please don't. Let's just say I don't like him because of the quotes; I like him in spite of them."

"I could serenade you instead." Chase sang the first few stanzas of "Twisted Transistor" by Korn, in the sweetest baritone ever.

waiting for it

"Hauntingly disturbing." I did like his voice, though. In fact, everything about this evening was pretty much perfect.

<hr>

The faint strains of "Heathens" by Twenty-One Pilots infiltrated my dreams and dragged me awake. I forced myself to sit. The only custom ringtone I had, because Lyn, Sadie, and I all had the same songs for each other.

"'S'wrong?" Sleep lined Luke's question.

"Nothing. Call from my friends. I need to get this." What was I supposed to tell them? Would they hear the shower running in the background? *Oh yeah, that's Chase. No big deal. Hey, did you know your brother is hung like—*

No reason to give them that level of detail. I'd be surface-level honest.

I raked my fingers through my hair, and pulled on a camisole as I dug my phone out of my purse. "Hey," I finally answered.

My best friends' faces smiled back at me. "We wake you?" Sadie asked.

"It's only six here. I'm surprised you're up before ten," I teased.

She stuck her tongue out. "We were promised secrets. Now that we're face-to-face, spill."

"It's not a big deal." Saying that, instead of telling them made it sound exactly the opposite, didn't it?

A door squeaked behind me.

"Do you want to build it up some more?" Lyn asked. "Add a few more qualifiers?" Her tone was light.

I let out a nervous laugh. "No. So here's the thing—"

"Hey, guys." Chase pressed into my back. His chest was hot against my exposed shoulder blades.

My stomach dropped into my shoes, as I stared at two faces working their jaws. This wasn't the way I wanted to tell them. "There was a fuckup with our reservations, so Chase let us crash with him."

That was innocent enough. Except the memories summoned by his fingers dancing along my waist were anything but.

"That was why you forgot to tell us you landed?" Was Sadie's tone flatter, or was I just expecting it to be?

The tiny image of me in the bottom right corner of my screen showed Chase, waving. "That was our fault." His tone was light and casual. "We distracted her by telling her how desperately we want her."

Really?

waiting for it

"*God*, could you not?" Sadie's retort reminded me this was normal for us. Chase had been doing this to me for years. He'd make a flirty comment, she'd tell him to stop, and I'd write it all off as Chase being Chase.

Except I knew better now. They hadn't been throwaway comments on his part.

"Wait. *We?*" Lyn said.

I glanced at Luke, who was sitting in bed, watching the whole exchange silently.

"Do you… Should I…?" I didn't know how to phrase my question.

Luke nodded. "I trust them to be discreet." Rinslet had a barely-existent fraternization policy, but a manager fucking a direct report was still frowned upon.

I turned my camera toward him, and he wiggled his fingers.

"Is that… *Score.*" Lyn's enthusiasm sent pleased embarrassment rushing through me. "Is this a dating thing?"

This was awkward from both directions. My friends had metaphorically walked into the bedroom the morning after, before the guys left, and plopped down on the bed to ask for details. And the guys stuck around to listen. "Kind of. Yes. I mean, not like Sadie's thing."

"A test drive. I get that." Lyn sounded completely unfazed.

"Sadie?" I asked. Her silence and flat expression had me worried.

She shrugged. "You grew up together. Isn't that weird?"

Even though her question mimicked my earlier thoughts, defensiveness filled me. "So did you and Jax."

"True." Sadie's tone wasn't as convincing as I'd hoped. "I get it. I mean not really, because eww… but I guess if I weren't related, I could see the attraction to Chase. And your boss? Score." Her smile was a relief.

"That's what I said," Luke called.

This wasn't bad. Much closer to best-case scenario than worst. "So we're good?" I asked.

"As long as no one hurts anyone's feelings, we're fine." Sadie winked.

"And also, as long as you make time for us still between work and your fuck boys," Lyn added.

I grinned. "Deal. Talk to you soon." I disconnected and dropped my phone back in my purse.

Pleasant shivers raced over me when Chase nuzzled my ear. "Feel better, now that you have Moms' permission?"

waiting for it

"Could you not?" I mimicked Sadie's words from earlier, my tone as light as my mood.

Luke climbed from the bed to join us, and stood in front of me. "I like the idea of being a fuck boy. It's got a ring to it." He lifted my chin, and I met his gaze. "You were right yesterday."

"About what?"

"It's going to be hard to get any work done today."

My smile grew. The silly one that had flitted in and out since last night. "We'll manage. You have faith in me."

"Smart man." Chase settled his hands on my hips.

This was perfectly delicious. I could handle being sandwiched between the two of them over and over and over. "We don't *have* to go into the office, do we?" I let disappointment mingle with teasing.

"You probably should." Chase planted a row of kisses up the side of my neck.

I tilted my head, to give him better access, careful not to break away from Luke's touch. "Easy for you to say. You're not going with us."

"This went so much better than we planned." Luke murmured against my lips.

My laugh faded as his words sank in, dragging ice through my veins. "*Planned*?"

Chapter Fourteen

Behind me, Chase stopped moving. He felt frozen in place.

Luke pulled back to study me with concern.

"What do you mean, *we planned*?" Nagging whispers about potential definitions chewed at my thoughts, but I wasn't going to make any assumptions. I wanted to hear the truth. It would be fun. Funny, even. And then we'd go back to playful kisses and taking too long to get ready for work.

Chase moved into view, a reassuring smile on his face. He couldn't hide the hesitation underneath. "Nothing. We've talked before about how we're both attracted to you. *Planned* isn't really the right word for that."

"No, it's not." My concerns were growing, rather than rushing away. Shawn lied to me so many times when we dated. Cast so much doubt back on me. Made me question myself—my feelings. I never saw it until we broke up.

Was I missing it again?

waiting for it

Chase was a friend. So was Luke. They wouldn't—

"*Planned* is the right word for it." Luke sighed. "Calling it anything else is bullshit."

Nope. Nuh-uh. I would not jump to conclusions. "What is *it*?" I looked at Chase. "Tell me straightforward-like. Don't wrap it up pretty."

Chase pinched the bridge of his nose.

"When hooked up, your name came up," Luke said. "I'd tell you I don't know how, but you were there in every other tangent. It came out that we both like you. Care about you. Would like more than friendship."

That was sweet. So why did it taste rancid? "Okay?"

"I admitted I was holding back for the same reasons you hesitated—our shared friends." Chase pulled on a pair of trousers over his boxer briefs.

"Luke was hesitating because he's my boss." An explanation I was sick of hearing. Not because it was an invalid reason, but I didn't see a way around it, and that obstacle nagged at me. None of this eased how much the word *planned* bothered me. "And?"

Luke stood with his feet shoulder-width apart, hands clasped behind his back. "I had another reason for waiting, but it's related. You're not going to be working for me much longer."

They couldn't fire me, could they? "After everything I've done? All the hours I've put in? I'm on the chopping block?" I mean yeah, our game launch had been the worst in the company's history and I was a team lead, but I'd tried. My heart hammered against my ribs, and my breath came in short gasps. This wasn't—

"*No.*" Luke was emphatic. "No one is firing you. I promise. The opposite. You're not supposed to know this, but after the game launches, Scott wants to move you into a Design Director position. He's just waiting."

The wheels in my brain spun freely, not snagging anything. Not processing anything. Promotion. Not working for Luke, but with him. Recognition for the months of long hours. Having a say in the direction of games. My dream job. "Basically, everyone's just... waiting?" More motivation to finish the game. Like I needed another reason.

"Exactly." Luke's smile was tentative.

I should leave things as they were. This was a happy outcome. I mean, until I had to pick a guy, or things didn't work out with either of them, but there was no reason to go into dating assuming the relationship would fail. "But that's not what you mean by *we planned.*"

waiting for it

Chase winced. "We agreed neither one of us would pursue you until we both could. He made a move early, and I didn't want to miss my chance."

"And?" I wasn't hearing anything bad, per se, but they radiated guilt. The backstory was nice, but it didn't answer the original question. And why did Luke's phrasing make them look like they'd been caught with their dicks out?

"We may have made a bet about which one of us could win you over." Luke grimaced with each word. "The prize is you."

They made a wager, and I was the reward? My jaw dropped. Apparently that was a thing that really happened. I tried to find a response, but anything I would have said would sound more like a low keening than words.

"It's not like what you're thinking." Chase reached for me.

I stepped back until I collided with the dresser.

"It was a stupid way to phrase things." Luke hadn't moved from his at-ease stance. "I care about you. Not a stupid bet."

"Yeah, but you agreed to it anyway. Not only that, but you meant it enough that you still think of me in those terms." My voice came back, fueled by anger, hurt, and disbelief. "I can't— You really— A fucking bet? Am I supposed to be flattered that you think I can be won and traded? Spoiler alert—I'm not."

Chase took a step toward me. "Annie."

"No." I held up my hand, index finger out, as a warning. I saw two choices—curl up in a ball and sob for the next decade, or swallow this horrific feeling and go back to work. I wouldn't pretend none of it had happened, but I would ignore the giant pit in my gut that enjoyed any part of it. "Don't call me that. Don't touch me. Don't come near me. Guess what? You both lose."

"Please. I'm sorry." Luke's posture softened, but he kept his distance.

I grabbed a change of clothes from my luggage and focused on keeping myself from shaking. From breaking. Was the room part of their plan? This trip? The seat upgrade had been. How much didn't I know? "I'm going to shower. And when we get to work, I'm going to pretend nothing's different. And Jamie is going to spend the day finding me a new room."

"All right," Luke said.

I stormed into the bathroom, slamming the door behind me. I barely managed to get my clothes off before stepping under the shower. The water shifted from lukewarm to too hot, and I didn't care. I needed the sound to drown out any sobs that slipped out with the tears streaming down my face.

Chapter Fifteen

My eyes were clear and my resolve was steel when I emerged from the bathroom, ready to confront the day. Chase was gone.

Seeing Luke sent a wash of uncertainty through me.

"Anne…"

"Nope." I couldn't say more. Wouldn't bend to the doubt.

He sighed. "Give me fifteen minutes, and we can head into the office."

A little more time to compose myself. I'd passed that first hump of looking Luke in the eye again. I could do this. I just had to treat him the way everyone else did. Not like a friend or a crush or more.

I hadn't been here long enough to unpack much, so gathering my luggage didn't take time. A tiny thing to be grateful for that didn't make me feel any better.

Luke was my boss. That was it. He'd reminded me many times in the last few days.

Chase was probably going to be harder to shove aside, but I could focus on one thing at a time. After work tonight, I'd go back to my own room and probably not see Chase again until the week was up.

Easy peasy.

Another wave of sobs bubbled up in my throat, and I clenched my fist until it passed. I wouldn't cry over something like this. Last night was fun. I misunderstood the purpose, but now I knew, and I hadn't technically lost anything or anyone.

Not really.

Only two people I considered friends.

But once I recovered from the shock, we could be friends again.

Maybe.

Just not anything more.

An ache pinged behind my ribs.

I could do this.

I didn't give Luke more than a glance when he finished his shower. Partly to drive home my anger, but as much to keep my resolve from crumbling.

Luke tried a few times to initiate conversation, but I didn't say more than was needed.

Rain drowned the world as we drove into the office. It mingled with the smoke in the air. Usually, I loved the rain, but today the news said the high

waiting for it

winds and lightning were increasing the fire spread and risk.

There was probably some sort of metaphor for my current situation in there. I wasn't going to think about it.

As we approached the building, I boxed up my hurt inside steel and ice. I'd spent years pretending I wasn't attracted to Luke. I could live on the other side of the coin, too.

We arrived before half the office, but Mike was already here.

Luke grabbed his attention as we walked in the door. "I need a room where I can meet with some of your people today without disturbing Anne."

"Sure. I'd like to be in those meetings," Mike said.

Made sense. They were Mike's people

Move you into a Design Director position. Luke's news echoed in my thoughts. I should be celebrating that. Doing giddy mental dances every time I thought about it. But I was stuck in the emotional mire instead. With Luke holding meetings, I'd have a while to ponder. That was good, unless I thought myself into a pit I couldn't climb out of.

Luke nodded at Mike. "Get me a room. I'll include you on the invites."

I turned away and headed toward my—our—temporary office. I was halfway down the hall when I heard Mike.

"Anne. Hold up." He jogged to catch up with me.

I gave him my practiced smile. "What's up?"

"Are you all right?"

"Totally fine. Why?" I was more out of sorts than I thought, if Mike noticed. He'd never struck me as an observer of people.

He shrugged. "Just an impression. I know everything is stressful right now. Trust me, I know. If you need an ear from someone who gets it…"

I wouldn't be talking to him. I forced my smile to reach my eyes. "Thanks. I appreciate it."

Maybe I'd misjudged him. From every other time we'd ever spoken.

I set up my laptop and tried to dive into work. After a few false starts, I managed to lose myself in admin tasks.

"Hey." Luke's tone was quiet when he interrupted a few hours later. "Lunch?"

I shook my head and kept my eyes on my screen. I'd walk down the street and grab something quick when he was gone. The more time I could spend engrossed in my work, the less I had to think about how Luke and Chase used me as a prize in a dick measuring contest.

waiting for it

"Before I go, Jamie's been calling around off and on all morning. She hasn't found any rooms yet, but she'll keep trying," he said.

I didn't want to keep her from her work. True, this was part of her job, but— "Don't worry about it." My voice was raw. "I'll sleep on the couch."

"A—"

I glared at him. "The couch is fine."

"All right." Luke left again.

I let out a long sigh and dropped my face into my hands. I hated this. Why did they have to… Why couldn't they have just… They could have just told me.

Then again, I could have done the same, instead of making assumptions and swimming in fantasy for so long.

That didn't make what they'd done any more right. I couldn't forget that. They'd bet me as a prize.

I turned my attention back to my laptop.

Well, *attention* was a loose term. I wasn't focused on anything. The email from Zane was a welcome distraction.

Rumor was, more than a decade ago, before the company was even known as *Rinslet*, he'd hacked their network and distributed a release version of a game weeks early.

He'd been hired to keep people like him from doing the exact same thing, and while this situation wasn't identical, I wondered if it ate at him that it happened under his watch.

His email might as well have been in a foreign language. I understood enough to know it contained computer names and IP addresses, but the rest escaped me.

I called him on my cell phone, in case I needed to wander to someplace more private. "Tell me what I'm looking at."

"Someone, presumably from Team Percival, hopped almost every development machine in the building, to connect and upload that content."

That didn't make any sense. Rather, I understood what he meant, but not why anyone would do it. "Indulge me and let me talk through this?" I said.

"Sure."

"Typically, a person hops connection points to hide their location." The concept was, as I understood it, to use one internet connection to get to another and another and another, until it was difficult or impossible to find out where they'd started. "Which means they wouldn't want all those points in the same place, and they'd prefer unsecured or at least less secure spots to connect to."

waiting for it

Zane clucked. "Typically."

"So why do things this way?" I knew the answer, but I didn't want to believe it.

"Because they either want you to know it was them, or they want you to think it was someone very specific."

That was what I was afraid of. "Don't we have security to prevent this?"

"Security only works if people aren't sharing passwords."

I wanted to ask my last question least of all. I saw the answer in his message, but maybe he'd tell me I'd interpreted things wrong. "Who does it point to?"

"Wilma Clayton."

Billie. The woman Mike indicated. One of our best Percival devs. It couldn't be what it looked like. But unlike people, data didn't lie.

If I told Luke about this, would he fire her on the spot? "I need time to investigate," I said. "Leave this with me?"

"I understand, though I don't like it. I am going to force that entire team to change their passwords, right now."

That made sense. "What do I need to do?"

"Email everyone. Tell them they'll be locked out of their machines in five minutes. They can get back in when they change their passwords."

I was already typing. "Done. I'll keep you posted on the Billie thing, I promise."

"Be right about this, Anne."

I wanted to give him a confident *I am*. The best I could manage was, "Talk to you soon."

Seconds after I sent the message, I had a reply from Mike.

What do you think you're doing? This is my team. You can't make calls like this. Are you an idiot, or just trying to steal my job?

The harsh words sank under my skin, and I was typing a reply before I could process. *I'm sorry. The decision needed to be made right away. I didn't mean to step on your toes.*

I hit *Send* and sank back in my chair. I'd made a mistake, but was it in asking Zane for more time, or in cowering with Mike?

Chapter Sixteen

Luke didn't take issue with my decision to force the password change. *I trust you.* His assurance didn't soothe me the way I think he intended. Why couldn't I trust myself?

On the drive back to the hotel, Luke called Chase. Such great pals, they decided which of them got to date which woman and had each other's numbers.

Luke put the conversation on speaker, *to make sure everyone was on the same page*, and told Chase finding new rooms was a bust, so he'd have roommates again tonight.

So much for avoiding Chase.

I didn't say anything. I didn't know if it would be worse if I let the anger flow and wanted to take it back later, or forgave them when I wasn't sure that was the right thing to do.

With Shawn, every time we fought, he'd insist it was my fault. For saying the wrong thing. For overreacting. For making him mad.

I'd figured out after that wasn't the case, but my fucking brain still wavered on how to spot when I was interpreting things wrong. Especially here and now, with *them*.

Back at the hotel, I set up camp on the couch, pulled on my headphones, and opened my laptop. If that didn't say, *leave me alone*, I didn't know what would.

Chase returned a short while later and stopped in front of me with a warm smile. "Hey."

I pointed at my headphones and stared back blankly.

"Annie..."

It didn't matter that my music mostly drowned him out. I saw his lips move. Saw them form my name. Heard his voice in my head. I clenched my jaw and stared at my computer screen again, refusing to look up until I saw his legs pass by and disappear into the other room.

I had to get over this, and now was as good a time to start as any. Work would distract me. Hopefully.

When I was talking to Zane earlier, I'd put the pieces together that, if someone used internal passwords to make their hops and release our spoiler info, they could have just as easily used Billie's info to frame her. The thought had nagged me since that conversation, and it was the biggest reason I hadn't looped Luke in yet. We should have fired Billie the moment I had the information, but my gut said not to.

My gut also said Luke would have listened to me, if I'd asked for time. But my gut lied a lot. What if I was wrong about Billie? What if I told Luke, and he fired her anyway, but she didn't do it?

I hated keeping this kind of secret, even though he'd lied to me. His sin wasn't corporate-espionage level; it was just Anne-is-gullible-and-fun-to-play-with level.

I didn't know where to start, to prove anything about Billie one way or the other. Her other work? On-network activities?

Like I'd done so many times in the past few months, I found myself staring at the version control system—the way we kept track of who was making changes to the code and what changes they'd made, in case we needed to roll back to something previously overwritten. This had very little to do with leaking a series spoiler, except that we'd split the details up between teams, so no one had the full picture.

Sure, someone could put the pieces together and figure out the full story—a lot of fans had done that—but a direct script excerpt? Something no one had full access to, unless they had administrator-level rights to source control? Which would include a person with their manager's password?

Had *Mike* been in here, poking at things?

I stared for hours, but nothing clicked. It all looked normal. Billie had accessed a large number of files, but they were all ones she should be working with.

My gaze drifted to the computer clock, and when I saw it was almost nine, my stomach growled. There were no answers for me here tonight. Maybe when my head was clearer.

Time to grab some food then pretend I could sleep.

I closed my laptop, set it on the coffee table, and pulled off my headphones. The moment I could hear the world again, the faint sound of the TV in the other room rushed in to meet me. It would be so easy to walk the ten or twenty feet to the bedroom, and talk to Chase and Luke. But I couldn't. What if I did that, and I set myself up for more of the same?

The sound of a door opening drew my attention, and I looked up to see Chase emerge from the bathroom. I traveled my gaze up his body, over gray sweatpants and his bare chest, to his damp hair and captivating stare. God, he looked good. The past rushed back in a wave of longing and desire, of staying with Sadie and always hoping for a glimpse of something like this.

waiting for it

Fuck, that hurt.

"I really am sorry. Talk to me, please," he said.

I wanted to. Wanted it so desperately that part of me was willing to accept and agree with anything he said, to make things right. That was the problem—I'd cave, and they'd think they could do something like this again. The way Shawn used to.

I shook my head, grabbed my purse, and walked out of the room. My heart dove into my empty stomach with a *thunk*, and my brain warred with itself. I was being unreasonable. But I wasn't. But I was. But... I grabbed my phone, more out of habit than because I wanted to look at it.

There was a text and a missed call from Sadie. *Call me. Stat.*

It was an emergency. I'd been moping in my own thoughts all night, and she needed me. I dialed her number, and pressed my phone to my ear as I stepped off the elevator.

"Hey," she answered cheerfully on the first ring.

"Hey. Are you all right?" I wandered over to a tucked away corner of the lobby.

"Yeah. Are you?"

What? I settled onto a cushion that let me press my back to a pillar. "You're the one who sent an emergency message."

"You're my emergency," Sadie said. "I'm worried about you."

Realization spread through me, drawing a sad smile. "You talked to Chase."

"He didn't give me details. He just asked me to tell you he was sorry. Said you wouldn't hear it from him."

No. My thoughts revolted. I didn't like the idea of someone playing messenger on my behalf. "I heard him fine."

"What happened?" Sadie sounded concerned.

Which—of course she was. I might doubt Chase and Luke's motivations, but Sadie was my best friend. My sister. "Apparently, there was more to this whole *hitting on me* thing than he or Luke disclosed up front." I laid out the conversation from this morning for her. Bile coated my throat when I got to the part about the bet, but I made it through the whole story without falling into tears of frustration.

"Basically, Chase and Luke went out, and it didn't go anywhere because they both like you, and they talked about that." The way she said it made the whole thing sound simple and trivial.

Wasn't it?

I bit the inside of my cheek, to collect my thoughts before replying. "They discussed competing against each other to win me over. They made a bet. And they never bothered to tell me."

"Telling you kind of invalidates the bet, right?" Sadie laughed.

I didn't know how to respond. She was agreeing with every part of me that said I was being dumb.

"Jax and Grayson talked about dating me, before they approached me," she said.

"Jax and Grayson were already a couple, and they didn't talk about you like you were some sort of prize to be won. They didn't establish rules. Contest terms. A bet, about who could steal your heart first. Chase and Luke might as well be cashing in skeeball tickets for me. I don't even know if they like me or just liked the idea of the competition." The moment I spoke the words aloud, they latched onto a fear I hadn't given a name. Now it was real. And gut-wrenching.

"I think you're exaggerating. And of course they like you, Sadie said."

Was I? Exaggerating? Why did I feel justified in my reaction in that case? "This is exactly why I should have turned Chase down. I knew everyone would take sides." My gut had been right about that. "I didn't think..." The next words were harder to say. "I didn't think you'd be so completely on his. I thought you'd give me a little bit of—"

"I'm not completely on his side. I can hear in your voice that you're miserable, and this morning you were so happy, you were almost singing."

"They used me as the wager." I must not be making myself clear. What wasn't I saying right? "If I tell Chase this is no big deal, that my feelings on the matter aren't important as long as he *didn't mean anything bad* by it, how's that going to help me feel better?" I'd love an answer, because she was right. I felt like shit.

"That's not—"

"What you meant. Right. Silly Anne, misinterpreting things. Blowing her feelings out of proportion." The retort scraped through me like razor-bladed claws. It spoke to so many of the accusations Shawn threw at me every time we fought.

"That's not what you're doing."

"Forget it." I didn't trust her to say any more, or myself to hear either of us correctly. "Chase is *actually* family. I get that." I almost sobbed on the words. "I understand. Bye."

The instant I hung up, my phone rang again. Sadie.

I ignored the call.

And the next three, as I walked back to the elevator.

waiting for it

Her text came in as I stepped into the waiting car. *Call me back, please? Talk to me?*

Maybe she was right about what she'd said on the phone. Everyone was saying *please* and *I'm sorry*, and I was ignoring them.

But Shawn did that to me so many times—ignored my concerns and insisted if I didn't accept an apology, it was my fault. Who was I supposed to trust? The friends who'd always been there for me, or myself?

It shouldn't be a choice I had to make.

Chapter Seventeen

I wasn't looking forward to spending another morning commute of not talking to Luke. Especially if it was followed by us, working in the same room together and not saying anything.

He was my boss. I still had to discuss business with him. That wasn't a big deal.

I also needed to tell him about my findings from yesterday. "I talked to Zane. He traced the leak back to an account." I kept my tone cool and conversational, as Luke drove toward the office.

"Who?"

"Billie."

This was when Luke would stop being so nice. Tell me I'd fucked up. That I was an idiot. Ask why I'd kept things from him. Why Billie was still working for us.

Luke glanced at me. "What do you think?"

All of my defensive responses lodged in my throat. "I don't think she's responsible." I reached for reasons why not, but I hadn't found anything concrete yet.

waiting for it

"Okay. I can't hold the dogs off forever, but I can give you until the end of the day. You don't have to give me a new name, but I do need a direction to point Zane in, if this isn't it."

Tension I didn't know I'd been holding drained from me, and I sank back against the seat. "Thank you."

"Fuhgettaboutit," he said, in a near-perfect Tony Soprano voice.

It would be so easy to laugh. To have fun with this moment. I just had to forgive him and pretend twenty-four hours ago—or rather, the events that led to the revelation of twenty-four hours ago—never happened.

I wouldn't be tossed around emotionally like that. Never again.

This felt different than Shawn's emotional manipulation, though. But I couldn't put my finger on how or why.

We arrived at the office, set up in the conference room, and dove into work. The bulk of the sound in the room was fingers, clacking on keyboards. The air didn't feel as heavy as yesterday. Maybe the smoke outside was clearing up.

My phone rang a little after noon, and sourness coursed through me. It was Lyn. Would this be a repeat of last night?

I couldn't shut everyone out of my life, and I'd curl up and wither if I pushed away another friend. "I'll be back." I managed to keep my voice steady as I pushed back from the table.

Luke nodded, watching me with an expression I didn't want to recognize as concern.

I took the stairs down, to organize my thoughts to the rhythm of my shoes, hitting concrete. When I stepped outside, the sunshine hit my face and sank into my soul. I paused outside the door and drank in the warmth.

This was a building on a block of assorted businesses, so there wasn't a lot of space to loiter in, but I found an empty patch of sidewalk away from the entrance, near a tree, and dialed Lyn back before I could fall into the fear that this would go badly.

"Hey." Lyn managed to pour sympathy into the single syllable. "How are you doing?"

"Depends on what you've heard."

"That Chase was a dick. That Sadie misses you."

I sighed and blinked back the sting behind my eyelids. "I don't want to make you take sides." I couldn't stand losing another friend.

"Are you hurting?"

So much more than I wanted to admit. "Yes. But don't hate anyone because of me."

waiting for it

"Because of *Chase*." Lyn's correction was emphatic. "Did he tell you this is your fault? It's not."

"No. He never said anything like that." In fact, neither Chase nor Luke had. They'd been trying to apologize.

"I don't hate anyone. I want you to be all right."

A lump formed in my throat. Such simple words, and they were choking me up. "What if I'm wrong to be mad, though? What if the only reason it's a big deal is because I'm making it one? If I let it go and moved on, everything would be fine."

"Fine for whom? What does your gut tell you?" Lyn *tsked*.

Lies. Always lies. "To be mad. To forgive them. I don't know anymore."

"So listen to it."

I rolled my eyes. "If you're trying to be helpful, you're not." So why was my frustration sapping away?

"You're fighting your instincts right now. I know you. If you stop telling yourself you're wrong, and start believing you're right, it's going to help."

"So I'm wrong to think I'm wrong?" I chuckled dryly.

She laughed. "I suppose yes, I am saying that. If you were home, I'd wrap you in a big hug. Until then, hug yourself and trust yourself. I do."

So did Luke. He'd said so more than once. "If you insist," I said.

"I do. How can I help?"

"I think you already have." I couldn't explain how, but I was feeling a little better. She made sense, even with such a short exchange. Lyn was amazing like that. "Thank you."

We chatted a minute or two longer, made plans for the weekend, and then she had to get back to work. I needed to do the same, but I wasn't ready yet. I had to sort out the wash of emotion clogging my thoughts. I leaned against the tree, eyes closed and face to the sun, until I heard a car.

I looked to see Chase parking a few spots away. I expected a clench in my gut, and there was a small one, but it was tempered by being happy to see him.

He approached, a plastic takeout bag hanging from one arm, and a drink holder with three cups of soda in the other hand. "Authentic Russian food. You can either eat with us or take yours and go somewhere else. I'll understand either way."

"Did you and Luke plan this?" The question popped out without consideration. I needed to know.

waiting for it

He shook his head. "I wanted to see you, and I thought this might get my foot in the door."

"Food. You thought you could bribe me with lunch."

"Not *bribe*, but sate. You always forget to eat, Annie."

True. "Lunch sounds good." And I could eat in the same room as them. I'd spent the last few hours with Luke. I didn't have to talk to eat.

Chase's smile was brighter than the sun and twice as soothing.

We rode the elevator back up and found Luke exactly where he'd been when I walked away. He smiled too, when I moved my computer to the side and accepted a takeout box from Chase.

Chase had gotten me *pelmeni*—dumplings filled with meat. We didn't have a lot of variety in Salt Lake, but Lyn was eternally trying new dishes and comparing them to the local places as experiments for her café, and we got to be her taste testers. These weren't quite as good as hers, but I was biased, and they were real close.

"I don't think I've ever had Russian food before. This is good," Luke said.

"The people who own the place are this great older Russian couple. Political refugees."

Not something I heard very often when it came to other continents. "Like, former KGB or something?"

Chase's smirk said he had a story to tell. "Like Romanovs."

What?

"It's my understanding that's just a name these days." Luke looked as surprised as I felt.

"Not to the people who hold it." Chase leaned in. "*Never* tell a Romanov they're just a name. So this man's grandmother, back when the wall came down, saw the balance of power shifting and decided it was time for her family to fill the vacuum."

And I questioned *my* decisions. "Bullshit."

Chase held his hands up. "Honest to God, this is the story they tell. So Babushka had acquired a long list of friends in her life—she was everyone's mother or sister or best friend—and she'd convinced several of the oldest and the youngest that it was time to rise up."

I could almost picture that in my head. And I could see Chase spinning a similarly compelling argument, if he decided that was what the world needed.

"Since we've never heard of it, I'm guessing that didn't go well." Skepticism filled Luke's voice.

waiting for it

Chase wasn't deterred. "It was going better than you might think. Problem was, one of the women in her rebellion-to-be was married to a KGB agent. This girl would have freaked if he tossed her surrogate babushka in a Gulag—"

"Not a thing anymore in the eighties," Luke said.

Chase rolled his eyes. "Send her to Siberia, then. Whatever. So I'm taking a little bit of artistic license."

I suspected he was taking a lot, but the story was entertaining, regardless. "What happened next?"

"So Mr. KGB went to the actual grandson." Chase looked pleased that I asked. "Told him what she was up to. He actually sounded concerned. She'd organized hundreds of potential-rebels through all the people she knew. KGB agent gave this man and his wife a choice—take Grandma and leave the country, or she would be arrested. They weren't as impassioned about the cause, and Mr. KGB offered them the paperwork they needed to get to the US without hassle, so they packed up their belongings and their grandmother, and left."

It was a good story. Had all the right elements—a heroine I could root for, an extended family who cared, and a sympathizer within the system. "How much of that is true?"

"That's the tale they tell. Who am I to question it?"

I laughed in spite of myself.

Even Luke was smiling. "You do know some incredible stories."

"Funny how none of them are about you." I didn't mean it to be an accusation, but as I said it, I realized Chase rarely told tales about himself.

Chase shrugged. "I'm an open book. You already know all my secrets."

"Obviously not." I hadn't forgiven the guys yet, and I wasn't letting anyone off the hook for a few dumplings and a fairytale.

"She's right, you know," Luke said.

Chase sank back into his seat. He radiated confidence, even when he was being poked with doubt and criticism. How nice would that be? "As if you'd say otherwise."

My insides twisted, and Shawn's voice echoed in my head. *It's your fault you're fighting. If you'd been nicer, he wouldn't have to say those things.* God, I hated that voice so much. Why couldn't I ignore it?

Chapter Eighteen

I wish you didn't make me... The mental Shawn-voice faded as Luke held my gaze.

"If she was wrong, I'd say so. That doesn't happen very often, though." Luke was talking to Chase, but he was focused on me.

"Fair point." Chase's agreeing with Luke silenced the voice even more.

I didn't want to think about me. "Tell us a story about you."

This was when Chase would bite back. He'd tell me *no.* To stop. That I was stupid for pushing the issue.

"When I was fifteen, I was at Jax's. One of the rare times I spent more than a few minutes at his house," Chase said.

I didn't know this story. If I did, it wasn't in this context.

"Something was peeking out from under the corner of his bed, and I was curious. New comic? Naked chicks? The glossy cover and hint of colors made me think it was the latter, so I tugged. *Nope,* none of the above. Naked dudes. Alone. With each other. With the biggest cocks I'd ever seen. Not a single woman to be seen anywhere, and trust me, I looked. I stared at those pages and had no idea why they made my skin so hot."

Luke looked like he was trying to hide amusement.

I'd expected if Chase shared a story, it would be something lighthearted and flippant. That wasn't where this was headed.

Chase shook his head. "Jax came back from wherever he was—grabbing something out of the basement, or who remembers—and the instant I saw him, I shoved the magazine under the bed and ran back home. I was so embarrassed by my own reaction, I didn't talk to him for days."

"Is that why you pushed Sadie away from him?" I couldn't imagine, and the timeframe didn't line up.

Chase huffed out a laugh. "No. That was something completely different. I didn't understand how the pictures made me feel. It took me a while to process. That it didn't mean Jax was interested in me. That I could like girls and boys. That I could be turned on by them and still daydream about you." He locked his gaze on mine.

Heat flooded my face, and I turned away. I didn't want to feel better around him and Luke, but

waiting for it

I did. This was how it always went with Shawn, though. Wasn't it? We'd fight. He'd apologize and be sweet. We'd start over.

Why did this feel different? Not so littered with landmines?

We wrapped up lunch, and Chase left us to work. He'd convinced our vendor to accept our new deadlines and requirements, and was off to try to sign someone new while he was in town.

I only had a few hours left, to keep Billie from being fired. She probably had no idea—at least I hoped she didn't. My mind was clearer than it had been since we arrived, and now was the perfect time to go back over all the information I had.

Big problem was, I didn't have any more idea of where to look than yesterday. I stared at the source control, willing it to give me answers. All those files, ones Billie *should* be working on, checked in at seven. Eight, Mountain Time, since that was what my computer was set to, and those times made sense. We'd all been working late hours, and checking a file in at seven at night was nothing, comparatively speaking.

My brain clicked, whirred, backed up, and replayed what I was looking at.

Those were morning timestamps. "When did the leak happen? What time?" I asked Luke.

He half glanced at me. "We were on the plane, so… between eight and nine?"

"Our time."

He nodded.

"You ever talk to Billie before ten?" Now I had his full attention.

"Mandatory meetings, but no, not really."

It couldn't be this easy.

Why would someone do that? I'd asked Zane.

Because they either wanted you to know it was them…

Or were arrogant and didn't think they'd be caught. Not what Zane had said, but I could see it. I dialed him on the speaker phone between us.

"This is Zane."

"It's Anne. I need some information."

Luke was ignoring his laptop and watching me with curiosity.

"Shoot," Zane said.

This wasn't going to pan out. I'd need to go a different direction. "Who was in the office before eight—seven local time—Tuesday morning?"

"Mike Mejia, Jon Shepherd, Greg D'Angelo."

Not a long list, but I didn't expect it to be. "Dropping a list of dates in messenger. Looking for a common name among them." I gave him ten dates that fell before we had big code breaks, including

waiting for it

the major one that first delayed our launch, months ago.

While Zane typed, I forced myself to breathe. I didn't dare look at Luke. I didn't need another layer of stress added to this.

"Mike." Zane spoke with certainty.

"Thanks. I'll keep you posted." I hung up.

I finally turned to Luke again when he sighed. "What are we looking at?"

It was too obvious. Too easy. Why hadn't we seen it before? Because we didn't want to think one of our own would turn on us. This project meant everything to all of us.

"Mike is behind a lot more than a leaked ending," Luke said.

Maybe. "It's all circumstantial, and we'd have to do an audit on the code, to see if there's more to it than meets the eye. But the leak… signs point to him. What next?" I'd been taking stabs in the dark to get this far. "You can't just fire him, any more than you fired Billie."

"True, but I can talk to him. Do you want to be there?"

"Do you think I should be?"

"I think I'd like your opinion on the matter, but ultimately it's up to how comfortable you are with the whole thing."

I didn't want to look Mike—or anyone—in the eye and ask if they were involved in trying to destroy our project. But I had to know. If one of them was responsible, I had to ask him *why*.

"I'll be here." However, I would let Luke do most of the talking. I needed to absorb. Take my cues from him. Make sure my shitty instinct didn't speak out of turn.

Luke called Mike in first. If we felt like he was okay, he'd be involved in our conversations with the two people on his team. My gut told me he was where we needed to start, and that made me nervous.

"Hey." Mike smiled when he walked in the room. He settled into a seat a few down from Luke and never looked at me. "Manager pow-wow? We gonna discuss before Ms. Fortier pulls another power play, like yesterday?"

"Something like that." I couldn't hide the sarcasm in a retort I didn't mean to say out loud.

Mike didn't so much as flick a glance at me. "I understand that someone without a lot of experience makes bad calls sometimes. It's not her fault. But yesterday's stunt is going to cost us days of sifting through the fallout. Days we don't have."

Fury mingled with doubt. I hadn't fucked up, but that didn't stop the Shawn-voice from asking, *Didn't you?*

waiting for it

"No, it won't." Luke's tone was hard. "Anne made the right call, and no one's life fell into a downward spiral because they had to change their password."

Mike pursed his lips. "You're the boss, which is why I'm here. What can I do for you?"

"We're looking at the storyline leak that happened the other morning," Luke said.

Thank God he was stern and cool, because my doubt was clashing hardcore with my knowledge.

Mike nodded. "The information that came from Billie's account."

"It looks like that on the surface, but we don't think she's the culprit. Which is why Anne made the call she did yesterday." Luke's expression was marble. A Greek god, carved wearing a modern wardrobe.

Mike maintained a faint smile, but it didn't reach his eyes. "I'll talk to her about our security protocols and get something written up with HR. I suspected she was sharing her login information, to make her job easier."

He was awfully quick to cast blame in a specific direction. My irritation grew, drowning out anything else.

Luke shook his head. "I'll take care of that. Thank you. I'm more interested in the fact that the leak happened before she entered the building.

Early enough that only three of you were here at the time."

The way Luke was handling this was sexy. I'd like to think I could be as direct, but I'd probably waver. Especially with the way Mike was blocking everything with misdirection.

Mike shrugged. "I assume she logged in from the VPN."

"The leak came from within the building. Internal IP address, not a VPN connection." I was tired of this. Mike had flaws, but he wasn't stupid. There was no way he thought we were buying his story. Did he want to be caught?

The asshole still didn't look at me. I slammed my palm on the table, sending a sharp *smack* through the room and making him jump. Good. Arrogant fucker. "We need to know you're not responsible for the leak." My voice was harder than I expected.

Mike finally turned toward me with a snort-laugh. "You sure do like to jump to conclusions. Why would I do that?"

"I don't know. Why?" I bit back. His confidence made my doubt return. Why were we doing this? He couldn't be guilty.

Mike narrowed his eyes. "I suspect whoever did it found out what a bullshit ending we're about

waiting for it

to be fed, and wanted the world to know how badly you fucked up."

"*Chloe* has known how this series will end since Game One. And it's a good fucking ending." Now I was getting defensive and swearing. I needed to yank my emotions back in, but I couldn't. "It's incredible. Just because your tiny, homophobic, incel brain—" I snapped my jaw shut, but I'd already gone too far.

Mike's infuriatingly subtle smile was back. "It's bullshit, and people like you are the reason the industry—this company—are in decline. You vapid—"

"*Enough*." Luke stood.

"*Why*?" Mike mimicked my earlier question. "People like her are the reason—"

Luke stepped closer to Mike and leaned in, palms on the table, silencing him. I'd never seen Luke look so terrifying. Or so incredible. He stared down Mike, their faces inches apart, but never touched him.

"Anne, call Zane. Tell him to lock down all the machines in the building *now* and completely remove Mike's access. When you're done, explain to everyone that they'll be allowed back in soon, and ask them to please stay at their desks until I can talk to them. I'm going to make sure Mike has his belongings and see him to his car."

I wanted to say *yes, sir* and salute. Luke's presence evoked that kind of reaction in me. His command of the situation was fucking sexy. "Will do."

"I'll fucking sue you and this entire company for this." Mike glared daggers at Luke as they left the room.

I made the request with Zane when they were gone. As I headed into the main room, I heard a quiet wave of *what the—?* roll through the cubicles.

"Everyone sit tight. We'll explain soon," I said.

No one heard me. Even the people sitting closest to me didn't look in my direction.

"Excuse me." I raised my voice.

Heads turned toward me, but not many. The volume in the room grew, as more and more of them stood to talk, and saw Mike boxing up his things.

"What's going on with Mike?"

"Are they firing all of us?"

"This is bullshit. After all the work we've done?"

The questions and fear grew louder with each passing second. This needed to be under control. Why did Luke make me do this?

Because he trusts you.

Right.

waiting for it

I climbed on the nearest desk, ignoring the *creak*. It held. "*Hey*," I shouted.

Two dozen people swiveled to face me at once, and embarrassment flooded my cheeks. I might be bright red, but I was going to do this.

"No one in this room is being fired. Not today, and God willing, not at all." This wasn't what I was supposed to say, but if I didn't do something, there was going to be a revolt. "Mike is no longer with the company. I know many of you consider him a friend, and this is never the way we want things to go. But Luke will explain everything in a few minutes."

"What happened?"

"Why can't we get into our computers?"

"I have unsaved work."

The shouts came from multiple places in the room, making it difficult to tell who most of them were from.

"Mike is a good guy."

"He was set up."

"You can't fire him because you're incompetent."

The last one sent ice spilling through my veins. The noise was reaching a volume that buzzed in my head and made it difficult to think.

Chapter Nineteen

Billie stood next to me, stuck two fingers in her mouth, and released an ear-splitting whistle. "*Hey*. STFU and listen to the boss."

Did she really just say *STFU?* I liked her more than before and could see exactly why Mike didn't. He probably hated that some woman had the nerve to speak her mind. His loss. I gave her a grateful smile and turned back to the room. "Yes, Mike's been let go. You all know Luke is a full-transparency kind of guy, and he'll fill in the details. As far as I know, no one else needs to be concerned. We just need you to sit tight for a few minutes, until Luke is back."

More murmurs rolled through the room, but they were of curiosity, not anger. The group's fear faded.

When Luke returned, he didn't offer much more information, but said as soon as he had clearance from Legal he'd explain more. It calmed people down, but I doubted anyone would get much programming done.

waiting for it

I was emotionally numb by the time we got back to the hotel. Between a fun lunch with Luke and Chase, and the turmoil with Mike, I didn't dare feel anything. I shrugged off Chase's offer for dinner later, and settled into my little corner on the couch, my headphones on.

Minutes ticked away on the clock, and I wasn't focusing. I tried pulling up a movie, but it didn't hold my attention. I avoided social media, because I didn't want the reminder that things weren't right with Sadie.

I wanted to be talking to my friends again. When I took off my headphones, voices drifted to greet me.

"… without Anne," Luke said.

"And when she's talking to us, we'll include her. This is about you and me." That was Chase.

What were they talking about?

"We were stupid to even consider it," Chase said.

"I think we've figured that out already."

Chase choked off a laugh. "I mean, in addition to the obvious *this was probably a bad idea*. It's killing me, to have her not talking to me.

"Same."

I shouldn't eavesdrop. I stood to join them and interrupt, but curiosity kept my feet glued to the floor.

"What would have happened if things went the way we thought?" Chase asked. "We both try to win her heart, and she picks one of us."

Anger tickled my senses at the reminder that *betting Anne's heart as a prize* was a real thing. I'd rather be dryly amused that they hadn't considered the potential consequences—any of them—sooner.

"To be honest, I never thought beyond a future with her." Luke sighed. "She'd end up with me, so there was nothing to consider."

"Except you're wrong. She'd pick me. We know each other better."

Nope, anger was winning out.

"Fuck, we're assholes." Did Luke sound genuinely remorseful? Then again, hadn't both of them before now, too?

"You know, I don't want to see you miserable almost as much as I don't want to be miserable," Chase said.

That was convoluted. I stepped up to the doorway and coughed, to draw their attention. "I'm not choosing either of you." The meaning behind the words, that I'd lose them both, clenched around my heart.

From the way one corner of Chase's mouth tugged up, he didn't reach the same conclusion. "That's my point. If you and I are together, I don't

waiting for it

have an issue with you and Luke being together too."

"I'm on board with that," Luke said.

I was too. Or I would be, if this one argument hadn't had so much fallout. "Too bad this was over before it started." I didn't know how I kept my voice from shaking, because the statement threatened to rip me apart. I couldn't talk to them anymore. I turned away.

"Anne." Luke's tone made me pause. "Do you ever wonder if you're doing the right thing?"

A shiver ran through me, and I resisted the urge to hug myself as doubt poured through me.

"This isn't me being passive aggressive or telling you you're wrong. You're not." Luke was kind. "I saw how you reacted to Mike. I felt your doubt, wondering if you were wrong. I've been there. I wouldn't be begging for your forgiveness if I didn't realize I'd fucked up. But I'm asking if you've got that voice in your head that belongs to someone else. The one that makes you question everything."

He was trying to manipulate me. To trap me into saying something I didn't want to. "Doesn't everyone?"

"No. But a lot of people do." There was an ache in Luke's voice that I rarely heard and never for more than a breath. "*I* do."

Did I dare ask? "How?"

"My first few weeks of college, I struggled to integrate. Mostly because I'd just come out of Afghanistan and was adjusting to things like sleeping in beds. Then I met the RA in my dorm. Gorgeous man. Sweet. Sure, we fought sometimes, but that was always my fault. He said so."

Luke stared past me, as if he was lost in a memory. "He was caught for dealing Adderall and blackmailing several of the people in the dorm. When he went before the disciplinary board, he convinced them it was my idea. He got us both kicked out of school."

I knew Luke didn't graduate. A lot of people at the company hadn't, because Scott valued skill in his developers more than a degree. I'd never imagined it hadn't been Luke's choice. I didn't know what to say.

Luke let out a shaky breath. "He apologized. Told me he was worried about his career. I understood, right? Besides, if I'd been more attentive to him, it never would have happened."

I knew this story. Not the details, but the ex-boyfriend's accusation. "But it wasn't your fault." I felt stupid, saying that. Luke had obviously figured that out.

He shrugged. "I'm lucky that I'm smart. It was enough to get me an internship at Rinslet, even

waiting for it

without the degree. I wouldn't be here if it wasn't for Scott."

That wasn't fair to Luke. "You wouldn't be here if you weren't intelligent and talented."

"That too." Luke grinned. "It's taken a lot of time and a bit of therapy to understand it wasn't me; it was him who was the problem. I still hear his voice, though."

"I know, Sadie knows. We all saw that Shawn did the same to you." Chase finally spoke. He turned from me to Luke. "And I'm sorry you went through that. I only know what it looks like from the outside, and that's hard enough. I can't imagine being in it."

My friends had tried to tell me then, and I'd pushed them away. Even if this wasn't the same situation, I didn't want to shove my friends out of my life again. "It's different."

"Because you recognize that it happened? Because you got out? Because he was right, and you're still wrong? Why?" Luke asked.

I didn't know how to answer his questions. I wasn't sure what was up or down anymore.

Luke frowned. "This bet? I was wrong to make it. Chase was wrong. You're not wrong for feeling anything you feel about it."

I didn't know how to sift through my thoughts anymore. They were a jumble of chaos. "That's sweet of you to say, but… you're wrong." I cut off my laugh at the twisted irony of my statement. "Good night."

Chapter Twenty

"Annie." Chase's tone stopped me in my tracks. "Don't spend another night on the couch. Take one of the beds. Better yet, stay and talk to us. If I have to promise I'll never tell you again how gorgeous you are, to get you to talk to me, I will."

I turned, scrunching my nose in distaste. "I'm not good with that."

"Which part of it?" Sincerity radiated from his expression. "How about, I can still shower you with compliments, and you can go back to pretending you think it's harmless?"

How did I ever do that? "None of what's happened this week gets undone. I want our friendship back, but I can't forget."

"Good. Because not all of this was bad," Luke said. "Not to me."

I leaned against the doorframe and jammed my hands in my pockets. "It only took the one bad thing to sour it all. But I won't forget the good either."

"If you want another apology, I'll give you one. Over and over." Chase looked so sweet. The boy next door. The guy I would have given my heart to years ago, if this were a movie.

I didn't want more apologies. "I get it—you're sorry. I can't say *it's okay*, because it wasn't. But I do forgive you." When the words rolled out of my mouth, they took a huge weight with them that I hadn't know I was carrying. God, that felt good. It couldn't be wrong if it was this much of a relief.

"Sure you don't want one more apology?" A hint of playfulness leaked into Chase's question. "Me, on my knees at your feet, worshiping you?" He stood.

Luke grabbed the back of his shirt and yanked him back to the bed. "That's not an apology; it's oral sex."

"The two are frequently the same," Chase said.

"Not when we're apologizing for objectifying her."

I couldn't help my smile as I pulled out a chair from the desk and sat. "I could stay for a little while longer. It's not like I was getting anything done, all the way out there in the other room."

"You haven't eaten yet, have you?" Chase was abruptly serious.

I shook my head.

Luke raised his hand. "Question. I've been wondering this for a while, and I can finally ask— what's your obsession with feeding Anne?"

waiting for it

Obsession…? I'd never thought about it like that before.

"Did you consider tackling that asshole you fired today, when he came at her verbally?" Chase asked.

Now I knew what they'd been talking about when I wasn't listening. War stories from the conference room.

Luke looked at me. "I not only considered it, I ran a split-second list of pros and cons, and I'm still tempted to find him and punch him for the way he treated you."

The protectiveness in his body language and words made me feel gooey inside. "People say things like that to other people all the time." Shitty, but true.

"But he said it to *you*." Luke told me before turning back to Chase. "What does this have to do with food? Did someone beat up Anne's food once?"

"You okay with me telling this story, Annie?"

Chase's question triggered a rush from the past when I realized what he was asking. I was touched that he wanted my permission. "Here, yes. Nowhere else." Everyone who mattered, except for Luke, already know about this part of my life. I didn't know if I could tell the tale myself.

"Annie's a fairytale princess, but Grimm got her origin story a little mixed up."

"I buy it," Luke said.

I'd never thought about my life that way before. "I'm not."

"Her mother passed away and left her to be raised by an evil stepfather." Chase slid into storytelling mode with his typical ease. "Down to the fact that he was the perfect member of the community in public. Everyone loved this dude."

"Ah." Luke frowned.

The wounds from my mother's death were old—I was only nine when it happened—but they still ached like a broken bone on a cold night. The memories of how my stepfather treated me were fresher, because I'd been stuck with him through my teen years. He was the reason I'd spent so much time at Sadie's.

"Half the time, the asshole didn't care where she stayed. That's why Anne's part of our family," Chase said. "The rest of the time, he needed proof that he was a loving father. For parties, social events—whatever. So she'd have to go home for a few weeks at a time."

A shudder raced through me, and I hugged myself. It was harder than I'd expected to dive back into this.

Luke furrowed his brow. "Are you all right?"

waiting for it

"I'll stop. You don't need to relive this." Chase looked concerned too.

"It's okay. Keep going, or you won't get to the happy ending." I had to remember the story had one. It was one of the things that kept me from falling into darkness when I looked back on that part of my life. "I wasn't abused or anything. Not physically. But there were a lot of nights I went to bed hungry, and to school the same way the next day. I learned to push through it."

Chase was shaking too, but his looked more like barely controlled anger.

"When Chase realized what was going on, he went out of his way to make sure you ate," Luke said in understanding. "Hard to compete with that."

"I thought you both agreed this wasn't a competition. Besides, I lo… ike you for different reasons." That was almost bad. I didn't want to linger in the dark anymore. "Anyway, if Disney ever writes a gamer geek princess, they totally stole the idea from my life story."

Chase relaxed a little, but he still sat stiffly. "Can you imagine Pixar basing something on our lives?"

"Pretty sure I've seen that on Smut Central." Luke's cheer sounded forced.

The conversation drifted toward light and playful, but the long week caught up to me earlier than I expected. I stayed awake as long as I could, but the next thing I knew, I was waking up fully clothed and tangled with Chase and Luke.

There was a text message waiting for me, from Sadie. *Please talk to me. I'm sorry.*

Chase rested his chin on my shoulder. "Don't be mad at her because of me. She's your sister."

Anne's part of our family, his words from last night rang in my thoughts.

"Go call her," Luke chimed in. "We've got time."

I didn't want company for this conversation. Luke and Chase would give me privacy, but I needed a little extra space. I grabbed my key, made sure I was presentable for the public, and headed into the hallway. I walked as I dialed and waited for Sadie to answer.

"I'm sorry," she said when she picked up. "For diminishing your feelings, for telling you that you were wrong, and for giving you a bad haircut."

"Way to take the *oomf* out of any speech I had planned." Not that I'd had any idea what to say. "And you haven't cut my hair since eighth grade."

"It was a really bad haircut. I'm really sorry."

I stepped into the lobby when the doors slid open. "It hurt. A lot. What you said, not the haircut." I planned to forgive her, but she wasn't walking away without me saying my bit. "I've

waiting for it

always looked up to you. Even now. And to have you dismiss me like that…"

"Why?" Sadie asked. "I'm touched, but I'm a shitty role model."

"You never hesitate or doubt yourself."

Sadie laughed dryly. "I doubt myself all the time, and I make my share of mistakes."

"But it doesn't stop you from *doing*. You always act." I leaned against a nearby pillar, tucked away from view.

"And you're smart about the decisions you make. You think things through. You weigh the consequences. Don't be me. I love you for you."

Same thing I'd told Chase and Luke last night. "It sounds pretty smart when you put it that way."

"Because I'm brilliant," Sadie said. "Forgive me, please?"

"I do."

"Good." Cheer slipped into her voice. "As soon as you have days off again, movie marathon. Your choice. I'm buying… whatever we need."

"It's a date. Talk to you soon." I felt better as I disconnected. It sucked, not talking to my friends.

My concerns from the flight were back. If this was how badly friendships could deteriorate after one argument with Chase, what would happen if we hooked up again and our relationship went even further south? I couldn't handle that.

I headed back upstairs, and the guys and I rotated through the shower, getting ready for our days. The one thing I wouldn't miss about this trip was sharing a bathroom.

My goal for the day was to find out how much additional damage Mike had done. I had a strong suspicion he was behind a few of the delays we had with programming, but if I could prove it, it would also give us a direction to go toward fixing things more quickly

I settled in to work next to Luke, in the conference room. It was bittersweet, swapping conversation and jokes with him like we'd always done, but knowing that more was possible if I was willing to risk it. I didn't know if I was.

Based on what we found yesterday, I asked Zane to have his team compare all the timestamps from when files were modified from this building, versus when people were in it. He had a list to me by midmorning, and I started working my way through it.

New problem—for every file change on the list, the history that came before it had been deleted. There was no way to roll back or recover anything that was changed.

Fuck. I sank back in my chair, pulling my attention from my screen, and blinked to clear up

waiting for it

my dry eyes. When I looked again, Luke was watching me.

"Something wrong?" I asked.

He shook his head. "Enjoying the view. How about you? You're stumped on something."

"Yes."

He tugged my hand from where it rested near my laptop, and brushed his lips over my fingertips. "Magic kissing mojo?"

I started to laugh, but revelation stopped me short. "*God*, you're incredible."

"I know. What's up?"

I actually had the answer. "Get me access to the deleted change logs."

"If I had that power, I'd do it in the heartbeat. But auditors only. You know the rules."

"Oh." I slumped again. The rule made sense, specifically in instances like this. If someone could erase things and then erase the proof they'd done it, we'd be fucked.

Except, what good did any of that do, if I couldn't restore things?

"I can get you screenshots or an export of the logs," Luke said. "Just not access to the software itself."

And if there was something to fix, we could go through the right channels to restore it. "I'll take that. Duh."

"Sorry. Wasn't thinking. I was distracted." Luke winked. "One extract from Internal Audits coming up."

By early afternoon, I had a list of everything that had been changed—presumably all by Mike, based on a ranting email he'd sent us this morning—down to the single quote. What Mike had done was randomly tweak modules after they passed final QA. Over and over, across different nodes and projects. More than half the time, it was a female developer's work—a neat feat, considering he only had four working for him.

The cheers from both Team Percival and Gawain, when I told them how much time we'd just saved, probably could have been heard without a conference line.

"You're brilliant," Luke told me when we finished the update call.

I flushed under the compliment. "I didn't do it all myself. *Magical kissing mojo*, and all that."

"No, this is all on you. Fantastic job."

Months' worth of stress faded away, as I started to work through my own list.

Now, if only my personal life could be as simple as restoring a few corrupted files from the past and overwriting the mistakes that came after.

waiting for it

Except, had hooking up with Luke and Chase been a mistake? Any of it? That little voice said it was, but I didn't feel like that was the case.

Chapter Twenty-One

That night in the hotel room felt like the when we'd checked in. The way things always had with Chase and Luke, before everything fell apart. Dinner, laughing, and having fun. I didn't even try to keep track of the tangents, as long as I could follow them and each hop made sense.

"Annie and I are Dance Dance Revolution champions. As in, *official*," Chase said.

Luke looked impressed. "DDR? No shit. Like *Scott Pilgrim* level?"

Chase gave a short barking laugh. "He wishes he was as incredible as us."

"I had no idea."

"There are a lot of things you don't know about me." I wanted to keep my tone serious and somber, but I was enjoying myself too much. Funny how frequently that was a state of mind for me around these two.

"We all have a lot to learn about each other. But I'm not opposed to stripping away a single

waiting for it

layer at a time, until I can see it all." The way Luke dragged his gaze over me, I felt it in my core.

Chase adjusted himself on the bed. "There's a lot of innuendo there. Does that mean we're transitioning from learning about each other to sex?"

"That's a real weak transition." Not that I minded. With the hurt gone, my mind was happy to linger on our first night here. The need. The want. I swore my brain was whimpering *use me*.

Chase shrugged. "It comes with a strong follow-up. That's got to count for something."

"Are we keeping count now? Inches? Orgasms?" With each word, Luke ticked off another finger.

"I thought you two weren't competing."

"It's always a competition when it comes to sex," Chase said.

Luke leaned in closer, mouth inches from mine. "Not if my filthy baby doll doesn't want it to be."

The words flipped a switch, and my every nerve ending sparked to life, looking for stimulation.

"Wait. Are you competing with me about who's right?" Chase asked. If he had any idea what was racing through my head, he was an asshole. A glorious, tempting asshole who was dancing his fingertips down my spine, and talking as if this were the most casual thing in the world.

"You two are ridiculous." My voice was breathy, giving me away. If the flush to my skin hadn't done so already.

Chase kissed the shell of my ear. "But we're well hung."

"Are we talking length or girth?" Luke asked.

"If you're going to insist on keeping count, I'm strictly looking at number of orgasms."

"That sounds like a challenge." Chase teased up the bottom of my shirt to brush my skin.

Luke hadn't touched me yet, but the way he watched me... "Where do I submit my application?" he asked. "I like to think I work well within a team environment. As long as I'm in charge."

"I think the application process should involve a talent show." I was going to make them work for this at least a little bit.

"Would you like to be restrained or just worshiped?" Luke asked.

Either. Both. And then some. They were making it hard to draw this out. "Without using me as a prop."

Chase stood and tugged at his zipper.

"Without using anyone's genitals as a prop." I added quickly.

waiting for it

Chase pouted. "You're taking all the hard out of this."

Luke knelt at my feet and grasped my fingers. "There once was a proper lady. Who moaned when her boss called her *baby*—"

"Is that a limerick?" I was laughing. "It's horrible."

"Thank God you stopped me, because I had no idea how to get from there to you kneeling and begging."

"You didn't have a problem with it the other night." Chase didn't sound upset. "Are you sure I can't just show you how talented I am?" He reached for his zipper again.

I shook my head. "That's not part of the application process."

"What do you bring to the team, Ms. Fortier?" The way Luke said my name grasped a moan from my chest and tried to extract it.

I painted on my best *innocent* face. "I'm adorable."

"You are," Chase said. "But if we're taking team applications, everyone has to prove themselves."

"Let's be honest, the competition is pretty weak right now." I had no idea what I'd do that would be better.

Luke pulled me to my feet and set me in the middle of the room, like he had the other night. This time he left my clothes on, at least for now. "All right, DDR champion, you can dance. Show us your moves," he said.

Yeah, right. "I don't dance; I follow a series of arrow prompts on the screen."

"I think he's onto something." Chase sat on the edge of the bed, full attention on me. "Dance for us."

I had no idea what to do, so I swayed my hips and hugged myself in a slow, I hoped hypnotic rhythm. It kept their attention, so I must have been doing something right.

"You call that your *Sucker Punch*?" Chase asked playfully.

He was referencing the movie, and so was I. "I prefer *Baby Doll*."

"Me too. And I like the dance. It's got potential. I'd like it better if you took your top off." Luke's tone implied more command than suggestion.

I stripped my shirt off, never pausing in my *dance*. The pair of hungry gazes on me was fuel on the fire simmering under my veins.

"Jeans next."

I spun my back to them as I undid the button and zipper, then shimmied the denim down my legs,

waiting for it

my ass straight up in the air. I turned to face them again. No idea how my basic pink bra and blue panties were drawing that kind of attention, but I reveled in it.

"What do you think?" Luke was looking at me, but I was pretty sure he was talking to Chase.

Chase tilted his head, looking me up and down. "Stunning, but still too many clothes." He crossed the room, pulled out a chair from the desk, and moved it next to me. "Lose the underwear and take a seat." His tone was more playful than Luke's, but no less enticing.

Luke snapped and pointed at the chair. "You heard the man."

I did and was happy to comply. It was easy to keep up the not-quite-dance while stripping off my bra and panties, but there wasn't much seductive about sitting.

"Spread your legs. Show us that incredible pussy," Luke said.

There it was—the tingle of desire. I trailed my fingers up my thighs as I pushed them apart. It felt incredible, to be exposed like this. To be the focus of their desire.

"No." Luke clipped off the word when I traveled my hands toward my core. "You can touch yourself everywhere that feels good, except there."

My laugh was strained, but I could tease a little longer. Or was he the one doing the teasing? I skipped over the center of my pulsing need and moved higher, dragging my nails lightly across the back of my neck. Gliding my palms over my breasts. Lingering to squeeze my nipples.

Chase had shed his pants and freed himself, and was stroking while he studied me. He was so hard. So thick. I wanted to taste and feel him.

I slid my hands down my stomach.

"No," Luke warned, when I drew too close. He'd removed most of his clothes, too, and his erection stood straight up, lonely and tall.

I nodded. "I could help with that."

"You will, baby doll, but not yet. You're busy with yourself."

Which was fun, but my body ached for more. I scratched up the inside of my thighs, then moved back to my breasts, to play harder this time. Rolling my nipples between my fingers until my body was clenching from need, and I couldn't pinch hard enough.

My chest heaved from holding back. "Please?" Begging worked last time, and I liked the way it tasted. Being vulnerable for them. Letting Luke control how quickly things went.

"Tell me what you want."

waiting for it

"You. Both of you." My plea came out breathless.

Luke gripped his shaft and dragged his thumb over the head. "No. But you can make yourself come."

Fucking right, I could. I dipped my fingers between my legs, sliding two inside me and arching into the penetration. It wasn't the same as one of the guys, but it was still incredible. With my other hand, I found my clit. There was no more buildup or tease. I rubbed frantically, grinding against my touch, my hips thrusting in desperation.

I melted against the hardwood back of the chair, head tilted back and eyes closed.

"Watching is nice, but I can't keep my distance anymore." Chase's words blended with the fuzz in my head, rather than disrupting it.

And then his lips were on mine. His fingers at the back of my head, holding me in place.

When he pulled away, I opened my eyes to find him watching me with a look that stole any breath I had left.

"*God*, you're gorgeous." His words rumbled over me.

Luke was next to him and had rolled on a condom when I was otherwise distracted. He gripped my wrist loosely and drew my fingers into his mouth, to suck them clean one at a time, while Chase teased along my chest and arms.

Luke tugged me to my feet, slid behind me, and pulled me with him when he sat. His cock slid inside me, stretching me out and making me moan.

Chase stood in front of me, lightly stroking himself.

I was hungry for more of what I'd had the other night. Losing myself in the pleasure of being filled. I leaned forward enough to lick Chase's tip. Swirl my tongue around the sensitive skin. Let my senses dance to his groans.

He thrust into my mouth.

Luke teased me gently. A barely there touch over my breasts, my nipples, and my thighs. It was a new kind of torture, on the opposite end of rough. Faint and almost ticklish. It felt as good as everything else we'd done, though.

When Luke started to thrust in me, the movement jarred Chase from my mouth. He picked up on his own. I watched, fascinated and aroused, as he yanked his shaft, his eyes half-shut.

There was a power in knowing he was doing that because of me. That even though he and Chase dictated what we were doing, I had the ultimate control.

The jerk of his hips and staccato grunts said he was close. He shuddered, as sticky white ribbons

waiting for it

squirted across his hand. My chest. A splash along my leg.

Luke gripped my throat, and pulled me into him, increasing pressure and the pace of his hammering in me. My head swam, light and giddy. Wrapped in pleasure.

Chase knelt between our legs, and I whimpered at the sight. He licked along my slit, and had to be tasting Luke as well.

Fuck, this was hot.

Chase focused on my clit, sucking and writing the most erotic sonnets with his tongue. Ecstasy enveloped me, encasing me in a climax that rippled through me, starting with the clench between my legs and tingling all the way to my fingertips.

Luke was grunting too—I was vaguely aware of that incredible sound. Slamming against me harder. Frantically. His voice raw. His grip on my thighs tight. The shudder of his orgasm rumbling through him and into me.

As we slowed to a stop, I swore the world around us did the same.

"Everything about you is fucking incredible, baby doll," Luke murmured against the back of my neck.

God, I just wanted to live in this bliss forever.

And ignore that teensy nagging insistence that I could never have this again.

Chapter Twenty-Two

A girl could get addicted to waking up sandwiched between two men. But as consciousness rushed in, so did the reminder that this ended today. Especially when Chase extracted himself to shower. He had an early flight out. Luke and I would spend a few hours in the office before we left.

Luke dragged a finger over my lower lip, as he lay next to me in bed. "What's with the pout?"

"I'm going to miss this."

"It doesn't have to end."

But it did. The realization I had yesterday, when I was talking to Sadie, wouldn't leave me alone. "Not talking to you two sucked. This has been fun and incredible and a whole huge list of adjectives, but that just means the longer we drag things out, the worse it hurts when things don't work out next time."

"What makes you think that's what's going to happen?" Luke asked.

"It might, it might not. But odds are higher on the *might* side." I hated the reality of that. "With

waiting for it

Lyn, we made friendship work after. I need that from the two of you—your friendship."

"You have it. Always." Luke brushed his lips over my forehead, then pressed his forehead to mine. "I'm going on record as saying I want more, but I understand why you're holding back. I'm here if you change your mind."

I nodded, and pulled away before I could sink into the comfort and lose my resolve. I sat with my back to Luke and hugged my knees to my chest.

Silence settled between us. When the shower shut off, the bed bounced from Luke getting up. "Do you want to go first?"

I shook my head. I needed more time to collect myself. That seemed to be my mood of the week.

"I won't be long. Then you can hop in." Luke grabbed clothes from his bag and headed into the bathroom as soon as Chase stepped out.

Chase studied me when he entered the room. "You okay?"

"Just gathering my thoughts. Telling myself I can do with you what I did with Lyn."

He frowned. "I don't think Lyn loves you the same way I do."

My breath caught at the confession. The declaration. "Chase, I can't—"

"It's okay." He crouched in front of me and cradled my cheek. He traced his thumb along my skin. "I'm not trying to guilt or force you into anything. I'm here for you, however you need. I always will be." Chase's sincerity ached more than if he'd laughed the whole thing off.

"I know." And I did. Even when we were fighting, part of me always knew I had him.

He pressed his lips to my forehead, and my heart clenched. "I have a plane to catch. I'll see you back home."

I nodded, not trusting anything that might come out of my mouth.

Luke and I wrapped up at the office. There wasn't much to do, besides tell the team they were awesome and to keep up the good work.

We headed to the airport and boarded our plane without issue. Our seats were next to each other this time.

I settled into the window seat, and Luke took the spot next to me. One of my least favorite things about flying was figuring out where to put my arms so I didn't bump into rowmates, but I liked the connection that danced between us when his forearm rested against mine.

We didn't say anything as the plane taxied. I was becoming a master at ignoring anything uncomfortable about silence with Luke, but that didn't mean I liked it. The dip in my gut as we left the ground was now tied to the memory of the first time Chase kissed me. I was going to call it ButterfliesPlus. I should trademark that.

"You thinking about the flight in?" There was no accusation in Luke's question.

I should tell him to please kindly step the fuck out of my head, but I didn't mind that he knew me well enough to ask. "I'll probably never fly again without thinking about that, even if it did turn out to be a mistake." The last bit felt obligatory, but it also didn't feel true.

"Do you really believe that?"

Not even close. I wanted to. Logically, keeping Chase and Luke at arm's length was the best way to avoid all-around heartbreak. It was also the best way to avoid any potential we all had together. "You're going to read into this, and I wish you wouldn't, but I can't stop you. Would you really be okay, being with me, if I was with Chase too? If I picked both of you, instead of one or none?"

"Yes." Luke's reply came without hesitation. "I'm really okay with it."

I flexed my fingers on my knee, twitching for something to grasp. Needing to ground myself. When Luke tangled his fingers with mine, a shock of warmth and surprise raced through me. I could pull away, but this was comforting. It was right. I didn't want to resist.

How long would it take us to get back to *normal*? Did I even want to?

We kept the conversation to work-related topics for most of the flight, planning cleanup, laying out next steps, and daring to dream about when we were finally done with this game. I appreciated both that Luke stayed away from personal topics and that he rarely let go of my hand until we landed.

Compulsion and experience meant we checked our work email while waiting for our luggage. The world didn't stop turning because we were in the air. Most of the messages I had would wait until I was back at my desk, but the meeting request from Human Resources made me frown.

"I've got to meet with Scott." Luke sounded as confused by his meeting as I was. "I can drop you off at home."

I showed him my phone. "I'm heading straight to the office, if you don't mind me hitching a ride that way."

"That's fine." Luke's frown deepened. "Any idea what it's about?"

"I was going to ask you."

waiting for it

We could toss all sorts of speculation around, but we'd have answers when we were done with our meetings.

Dana, the Human Resources Director, led me into her office moments after I arrived, though I was early. She closed the door behind me, gestured for me to sit, and did the same. The concern etched on her face made me uneasy.

"How are you doing?" she asked kindly.

It didn't sound like a casual greeting—not with that tone—but I didn't have any other context. "Good. A little jetlagged. Looking forward to sleeping in my own bed."

"I understand." Her chuckle sounded forced, and her smile didn't reach her eyes. "It's always nice to come home."

"Yup. Sure is." I was a master at awkward silences by now, but she had a reason for calling this meeting. "What can I do for you?"

Dana leaned in, eyeing me with sympathy. "You're familiar with our company's sexual-harassment policies? And you know that you can always come directly to me, if you're not comfortable going to your manager? I don't want you to ever feel like you don't have a voice."

Super weird. Tension cranked through me. "I realize." It would have to be a fairly significant level of harassment, for me to something like that, but I didn't really deal with it in this job. Mike was the worst, and he was gone.

Dana looked less comfortable with each passing second. "The employee that was terminated the other day, Mike Mejia, was apparently guilty of more than you realize. He forwarded me some information this morning, and while I don't know how he obtained it, the content has me concerned for your wellbeing and happiness."

"Okay…? I don't know what you're looking for, so you need to tell me what you're concerned about."

She leaned back to look at her monitor, and clicked her mouse.

"If there was a lock on the conference room door, I'd bend you over the table right now, and find out if you're as tight as I imagine." Luke's voice was hollow, coming from her speakers, as if recorded on a poor quality mic.

All the blood drained from my head, leaving my thoughts spinning and my skin cold. I'd never fainted before. Would this be a first?

"Is there more?" My voice cracked on the question.

"No." Dana's face was bright red. "Was he talking to you? The company supports you. Rinslet is on your side, as am I. You don't need to put up with this."

waiting for it

"I'm not putting up with anything." How much could I say? We'd broken the rules, and I had to admit that, to keep Luke from getting in trouble, but this could get us both fired.

Was she looking at me with pity? "There won't be any repercussions for you if you want to come forward, but you don't have to. He was completely out of line. He's being dealt with."

"Wait. As in, right now?" The words sank in, and my panic spiked.

"Yes."

The meeting with Scott. *Fuck.* I wasn't letting Luke get fired for sexual harassment. At least, if we went down, we'd do it together. "This isn't right. It's not what it looks like." I stood and walked out of Dana's office.

"Anne, come back. Please."

I ignored her. I couldn't think of anything, except that Luke was about to be punished for us having fun. The elevator up to the executives' offices took an eternity. I cut a straight line to Scott's office, and didn't pause when his assistant tried to stop me. When I pushed into the room, Luke and Scott swiveled their heads to look at me.

"You can't fire him," I said.

Chapter Twenty-Three

Scott gestured to the farthest chair from Luke. "Have a seat. Do you want me to ask him to leave the room?" Scott nodded.

"No. Please don't." This was bad. Another consequence. This one possibly unrecoverable.

Scott looked at his watch. "You didn't talk to Dana for long. Did she explain the situation to you?"

"Yes. Can't we say the recording doesn't exist, since neither of us gave permission?" I spared a glance at Luke, who didn't look nearly as concerned as I was.

"This isn't court," Scott said. "The fact that the recording is illegal doesn't change what's on it. We're pursuing Mike for a number of legal reasons, but that also doesn't change this circumstance. Do you understand how this looks?"

According to Dana, it looked like Luke harassing an employee. "Yes, but it's not like that," I said.

waiting for it

Scott pinched the bridge of his nose. "I've heard this story before. I've told this story before. Luke's already given me his side of things, and it's exactly what I expected. He told me he abused his position and crossed a line, and none of it is your fault."

"Why the fuck would you do that?" I'd smack Luke in the arm if he was sitting closer.

"To protect you," Scott and Luke spoke at the same time.

I crossed my arms over my chest and sank in my chair. *Idiot.* Lovable, sexy, protective idiot.

Most of the time, it was easy to forget Scott had been running this company in one form or another for two decades. He tended to look and act as young as any of us. Today, the lines around his eyes and mouth were evident. "This is where you tell me it's not his fault; it's all on you. That he didn't threaten your job, and you were out of line."

"Are you serious?" I stared at him blankly. "Why would I do that?"

"Like I said, I've heard and told this story before."

"Then you're an idiot too." *Shit.* I didn't mean to say that out loud.

Scott raised his brows and stared at me.

I really called the head of our company an idiot. And I wasn't even done talking. "It was consensual. All of it. There was no power struggle. There was some seduction, but really, it's no fun otherwise." I could shut up anytime now, please. "None of that's your business. Point is, I'm not going to tell you it was all my fault, and it's not all his fault. We're adults, and we both knew what we were doing."

Luke looked like he was trying to fight a smile. Nice to know my babbling in vague terms about our relationship was funny to him.

Scott was still watching me. "Are you done?" he asked.

"Yes," I said sheepishly. "Please don't fire me. Or Luke."

He stared at me until I wanted to look away, but I didn't.

"I still can't have you reporting to him, if you're doing what this recording implies." Scott furrowed his brow. "No, wait. There's no implication there. It's really straightforward."

I'd like to curl up in a ball and die now. "We're not doing *that*. Not anymore. Not that it's any of your business."

"The details aren't. The *one of my managers is sleeping with his employee* breaks our rules."

"You're dragging this out a bit much." Luke finally spoke. "It's starting to look dickish."

What?

waiting for it

Scott's face cracked into a smile. "I could see that."

"Is there a punchline here?" I wasn't going to be someone's joke, especially after everything that happened this week.

Scott turned back to me. "This was supposed to wait, but circumstances being what they are… I can't lose either of you, but I also can't keep the report-to structure the same. Anne, I'd like to offer you a director position. You can't step into your new duties until this game is out the door, but if you accept, you report to me, not Luke, effective immediately."

It didn't matter that Luke had warned me this was being considered; actually hearing Scott make the offer stalled my brain. I had the sense not to ask things like *what?* and *are you sure?* But most other mental functions left me.

"Anne?" Scott prompted.

I shook off the shock. "Okay. I mean, *yes please*. That is… I'll take it? Whatever it is I'm supposed to say."

"*Yes* will do fine." Scott chuckled.

We talked over a few more details, and he promised me an offer letter on Monday.

"Go home, both of you. Details are none of my business." Scott fixed me with a pointed glare. "Take the weekend off. You've both earned more, but that's the best I can give until the game is in players' hands."

Exhaustion and relief flooded me, making my limbs feel like lead, as we headed back to Luke's car.

He pointed us toward my house. "Do you want to celebrate?" he asked.

"Yes, but no. Maybe something small. I want to save the big one until I'm actually doing the work."

"Sounds fair."

"This doesn't change anything else between us." I hated saying it, but the point needed to be pounded into the ground a few more times, apparently.

Luke twisted his mouth. "I didn't figure it would."

What else was there to say?

Chapter Twenty-Four

When Luke dropped me off, he insisted on carrying my bags inside, even though I argued that I'd be fine. The *thanks, see you Monday* we exchanged was one of the most awkward things ever, and I'd just had HR play audio of my boss telling me he hoped I was tight when he fucked me.

I closed the door behind him and sank to the floor. The last week made me intensely aware of how empty my house was.

Fortunately, friends were just a message away. I sent Sadie and Lyn a text, letting them know I was back and that we should hang out tomorrow. Celebrate my not-quite-yet promotion. They understood when I said I needed tonight for self-care.

I showered without having to work around anyone else's schedule. That was nice. I yanked on my most comfy T-shirt and PJ bottoms, without worrying about who might see me in them. And I pulled my damp hair back from my face in a terrycloth headband.

None of the motions distracted me from missing Luke and Chase. My actions didn't convince me I was making the right decision by pushing them away. I could call, and they'd probably make time for me. Both of them.

Why was I fighting this?

What if I'm wrong? What if people get hurt? What if I get hurt?

But what if I was right? What if being with them was right? What if the last couple of days were a glimpse of how incredible things could be, despite setbacks? Didn't it count for something that I loved them?

Love. My own admission caught me off guard. It was true, though.

My phone buzzed from its spot on the table next to the door, startling me. The text from Sadie said *knock knock.*

A heartbeat later, someone knocked, giving me my second heart attack in so many seconds. It would be Sadie and probably Lyn. So much for self-care. Not that I minded the company.

I opened the door, to find Chase and Luke on the other side. Hello, Heart Attack Number Three. Especially with the way they both looked me over.

Chase held up a plastic bag with steam condensing on the inside. "Dinner? You got Sadie's

waiting for it

message, I assume?" His gaze had stalled on my chest. So he was behind the *knock knock* text.

"You're going to bribe me with food, so you can stare at my boobs?" I asked playfully.

"Food… Money… Promises of amazing orgasms…"

Luke shook his head and tugged on my hair. "I like this look on you."

"You like any look on her," Chase said.

"Truth."

I stepped aside to let them in. "Explain?" I meant to say, *to what do I owe this unexpected but wonderful visit*, but my brain and mouth were out of sync.

"We figured, if you were planning on staring blankly at the TV tonight, and we were planning on staring blankly at the TV tonight, we could do it together." Luke made everything sound so reasonable.

"At my house." Duh, me.

Chase grinned. "You're the one with the amazing theater room."

"Which you talked me into." Why was I arguing? I was elated they were here. It was perfect.

"Not that you needed a lot of convincing," Chase said.

Luke grabbed the takeout bag from him. "And we brought dinner."

"Which we covered already." I set the food on the table next to my phone. "That's it? *We're here to watch TV?*" I'd be okay with that, but given how much I wanted me-time an hour ago, I wanted all the us-time I could have. How had I convinced myself, even for a day or two, that I'd be okay, ignoring the connection I felt with them?

"We're also here to win you over properly this time." Chase grasped my fingers and stroked his thumb over the back of my knuckles. "By telling you up front that we've talked about this, and you don't have to choose, but we're hoping you will and it will be both of us."

My heart skipped, and I let out a soft laugh. "So win me over."

Luke rested his finger under my chin and tilted my face toward him. He brushed his lips over mine in a touch so feather light, he took my breath with him when he pulled back to hold my gaze. "I love you. I don't know long I've felt this way. Is it cheesy to say, *since the first time I talked to you*? I think it's true. I want you in my life. By my side. We make an incredible team. And an even better threesome. Especially when you're caught between us, holes filled, moaning in ecstasy until your voice is gone."

Heat flooded my face.

waiting for it

Chase saved me from having to think of a response, by moving behind me and wrapping his arms around my waist. He nibbled my ear. "I *can* tell you exactly how long I've loved you. My fifteenth birthday, when you wore that gorgeous sundress to try to get what's-his-name's attention. *George? Bob? Dickhead?*"

"You've been holding out on me for more than ten years?" I didn't know if I should lean back or forward. Luke had a point—me, pinned between the two of them, was pretty perfect.

"I know *now* that I've been in love for a long time. Back then, I just knew you gave me awkward boners and I couldn't stop daydreaming about you."

"Hmm… yeah. That's *true* love." Despite my sarcasm, I struggled not to laugh. "This is how you win me over?" It was working. I was hooked on both of them.

Luke jerked a thumb at the food. "Did we mention dinner?"

"And there's the whole *confessions of love* thing," Chase added.

I couldn't hold the poker face any longer. "I love you both too. I can't shove that aside or pretend it doesn't exist. It takes too much effort, and I'll miss out on too much."

"Exactly." Luke pressed his mouth to mine softly at first, then deepened the kiss into something demanding.

I draped my arms around his neck, drawing my nails up his skin, and sinking into everything.

Chase trailed his lips along the top of my back, to my shoulder, nudging one of my top's straps aside. "Food's going to get cold." He didn't sound concerned.

"Fuck the food." I managed between Luke's devouring my composure via my lips.

Luke bit my bottom lip. "I'd rather fuck you."

"That's good, actually. I don't want to walk into the kitchen, to find you with your dick in a box of Pad Thai." It'd be funny… but also disconcerting.

"Unless that's your kink." Chase glided his hands under my top, to rest his palms on my stomach.

Luke's chuckle was muffled. "If it's got more spice in it than the cinnamon in apple pie, I'm not sticking my dick in it."

"I'm spicy." They made me feel like I was, the way my skin lit up every time they were around.

Luke kissed the tip of my nose. "You're scorching. But more like peach pie."

There it was again. I pulled away to look him in the eye, without breaking the connection to either man. "What is it with peaches? Is that a guy thing?"

"It's an *us* thing," Chase said.

Luke almost looked apologetic. *Almost.* "One of the things we talked about, regarding you—what your pussy would taste like."

Should it sting, to be reminded of what they'd done? No. They apologized. I forgave them. "You know now."

"I do. And right now I'm very much in the mood for more of the same." Luke hooked a finger in my waistband and snapped the elastic. He kissed down my chest, hitting my bare stomach when Chase pushed my shirt up.

Butterflies danced inside when Luke knelt in front of me. He might be the one on his knees, but I was happy to surrender full control to his whims.

Chapter Twenty-Five

Luke dragged my clothes down my legs. His lips on the inside of my thighs—the rough scrape of his five o'clock shadow—burned over me. He followed a slow, indirect path that made me squirm in anticipation.

Chase kissed from my shoulder up to my neck. He scraped his teeth over the sensitive skin and sucked. I couldn't squeeze my legs together, but every other bit of me clenched at the tantalizing sting. The little girl in me giggled, and a laugh slipped out.

"What's so funny, Annie?" Chase asked between bites and sucks.

"Chase Hughes is giving me a hickey."

I felt him smirk. "And that's just the start."

Luke licked over my slick skin, and my laugh melted into a moan. He pressed his face into my pussy, devouring me, groaning against my skin, and sliding up to my clit and back down several times. He thrust his tongue inside me.

waiting for it

God, that was incredible. I swayed on my feet, into his attention, careful to never break away from Chase.

Luke moved his fingers to my clit and played while he devoured me from the inside out. With Chase's hands on me and Luke's tongue inside me, the drawn-out pleasure was delicious.

My pleasure built slowly. Each time I started to clench, Luke eased up.

Until he didn't. He pressed in hard on my clit, and orgasm ripped from me. I ground into him, breathless and needy, until it all became too much and my body shied away.

Luke stood, pressing me back against Chase and keeping me upright. They were so warm. So safe. So completely fucking amazing.

"You're wobbly, Annie." Chase's tone was playful.

"Proof the two of you are incredible at what you do."

Luke nibbled my earlobe. "We have a stunning medium to work with."

"I hope you don't think we're done, because *God*, I want to fuck you." In a single, impressively fluid swoop, Chase lifted me into his arms.

I laughed at the sudden tilt of the room, hugged his neck, and buried my face in his chest.

He carried me into my room and set me gently on the bed.

Both of them stripped out of their clothes and rolled on condoms. It wasn't some sort of fancy dance, but I enjoyed the show regardless.

Chase knelt between my legs and kissed a lazy path up, to my lips. He claimed my mouth, swallowing my sighs as he glided the head of his cock along my slit.

He slid inside me with a long groan that felt as good as his thickness. My body lit up in response.

He thrust at a slow pace, pulling out almost to the tip, before plunging deep again. "How are your legs?" he asked.

Pinned to my chest. "Better."

"Good." He gripped my hips, hitting marks Luke had left and sending sharp stings of pleasure racing over my skin. Chase rolled onto his back, bringing me with him, only slipping out for a second before impaling me again. He glided his palms up my chest, to cup my breasts. "You're my absolute favorite sight. Always. But especially when you're flushed and smiling."

My skin heated at the attention.

"Just like that." He smirked.

I didn't care that he set a slow pace. It felt good to have him buried in me.

Where was Luke?

waiting for it

Chase dragged his fingers up my back, pulling me into him, and the mattress shifted.

Slick, cool fingers teased along my ass. There was Luke. He nudged my rear opening.

It felt different. Not bad, though. "I've never…"

Luke pressed his mouth to the hollow of my neck, behind my ear. "I told you I wanted to fuck every hole, baby doll. Do you want me to stop?"

"No." If I relaxed both my body and my trepidation, his touch felt good. "But be gentle?"

"For this, all right."

More cold slid over my skin. I didn't have lube in my house, though I would in the future. "You planned this."

"I hoped it." Luke barely penetrated me with two fingers. "I was a Marine—always be prepared."

"Those are Boy Scouts," Chase said.

"*You're* a Boy Scout." Luke's tone was teasingly defensive. "I mean, yeah. I think you're right."

My laugh mingled with a sigh. Luke pulled his touch away, but Chase was tracing his thumb along my slit, bumping my clit before gliding away again.

Luke nudged my ass again, this time with the head of his cock. "Relax," he said gently. "You're going to want to clench. Focus on doing the opposite."

Chase distracted me with licks along my chest, as Luke pushed into me an inch at a time. Slowly. Coaxing me. The stretch—the new sensation—was agonizingly delicious.

"You good?" Luke asked when he was fully inside.

I nodded.

The rocking between them was slow as well. A cautious buildup toward the incredible. Mild discomfort melted into pleasure, flowing over and through me.

As the speed of everything increased, my orgasm held back. Unsure what to make of this new combination of touches.

Chase finally focused on my clit, circling and rubbing. Harder. Faster. Pushing me past that edge of uncertainty to tumble into a ravine of intoxication. I dug my fingers into his arms when I came.

He moved his thumb to my mouth, and I sucked hungrily. Climax lingered, holding me in that cloud of pleasure.

I lost track of who came when. The room was a chorus of grunts, screams, and then heavy panting, as we slowed and struggled to catch our breath.

When Luke slid out of me, I felt like part of me deflated. He pressed against me, though, keeping me from missing his presence.

waiting for it

Chase softened inside me and slowly withdrew as well. "I was worried you wouldn't hear us out."

Luke kissed along the back of my neck. "I wasn't."

"Really?" I raised my brows, though only Chase could see.

Luke nipped at my shoulder. "Not really. I was terrified of losing you."

"You didn't." I couldn't imagine being this close to one of them and not the other. How did this happen in just a week? Or was that why I'd never dared admit either of them was flirting with me? Because it would mean choosing?

It's because you're dim, and you're wrong.

It was easier than it had ever been, to tuck away the Shawn-voice. It didn't belong here. "Though I'm grateful you didn't make me choose."

"Me too," Chase said. "You would have picked, but you would have always felt like something was missing."

Luke snorted. "You mean picked me."

I rolled my eyes, but I was laughing. That would probably become a new regular. "Doesn't matter now, because you both got smart."

"Damn straight." Chase tilted his head up, to brush his lips over mine, then rolled me onto my back.

We cleaned up. Or rather, they insisted I stay where I was, and they cleaned themselves and me up, then served me dinner in bed. Pretty sure they didn't plan this part, unlike the double penetration, because my being fed hot wings while surrounded by fluffy bedding, and trying not to giggle at the fun, was messy.

Which I loved. Then again, I loved all of this.

"All my friends are heathens—"

"Your friends are calling." Luke talked over my ringtone.

Last night, I slept better than in ages, and we'd all been awake for a bit this morning, but there was the sex, and the lying around, talking about breakfast, rather than actually getting it.

"I'll get it." Chase climbed from my bed. He looked gorgeous and very naked.

Speaking of—   "They're probably on Facetime." I didn't move to stop him.

"You get it." Chase tossed the phone to Luke, who was still covered by blankets, and pulled on his boxers.

Luke swiped to answer. "This is Anne's phone. She's tied up at the moment—"

waiting for it—

"Not literally." I poked my head into the frame, loosely holding the sheet over my chest. My hair was a mess. They'd seen worse.

Chase dropped back into the bed, on the other side of Luke. "Ladies."

Sadie covered her eyes and peeked out through her fingers. "We'll call back when you're not busy. This afternoon?"

"Probably a good idea, and that'll work." I laughed.

"But you owe us details," Lyn added.

Sadie screwed up her face. "Eww, no. No details."

"She can censor the story and just include the important bits about me," Luke offered.

Nope. I was going to be selfish about my men. "They're mine—the guys and the details. Sorry, not sorry."

Sadie rolled her eyes. "You can keep them."

"Lucky bitch." Admiration filled Lyn's voice. "Let's do lunch later. Bring your boy toys. We need to grill them. Question, not— You know what I mean."

"Question us about what? You already know us," Chase said.

Sadie shook her head. "Apparently not."

This was going to get circularly silly quickly. "'Kay. We'll send lunch details."

"You'll get distracted and forget," Lyn said. "We'll send lunch details, and if you're late, we'll assume you're fucking."

"La la la la la." Sadie mimed covering her ears.

That goofy grin was back. The one I had the day we arrived in Sacramento. "Love you both. Later." I hung up.

Chase took the phone from me, turned it off, and tossed it to the foot of the bed. "I believe we were discussing breakfast?"

"Anne à la mode?" Luke nuzzled my neck.

This was so right. The perfect fairytale ending, for this twisted princess.

Epilogue

It took four more months to get the game in the hands of our customers, even with all the code Mike tried to get rid of, and another two months to make sure everything was stable.

But here I was, in my new office, with my finally-official *Director* title. I sank back into my executive chair, a permanent smile on my face.

Billie had stepped into Mike's job in Sacramento, and now that I'd been promoted, she was leading both teams, though several of our developers were moving on to pre-production games. I was heading up one of those new projects, and while it wouldn't hit market or so much as tickle gamers' thoughts for years, I was so excited to have a say in it.

My office was a lot like Luke's, but in a different part of the building. A huge *CONGRATULATIONS* sign hung from the top of my whiteboard, and my trashcan was filled with paper plates, cake crumbs, and empty soda cups.

My desk was mostly clear, but a figurine of X, courtesy of a miniature sculptor Lyn knew, lived between my monitors.

And Luke sat in the chair across from my desk. "How do you like the new digs, Bosslady?"

"*Digs?*" It was weird, me being in the Director's chair and him on the other side of the desk. "They're swell." Weird, but amazing. Then again, everything with Luke and Chase was amazing. I was seriously smiling all the time.

"You usually say *swell* when things aren't."

Fair point. "This time, they're actually swell. I love the new place. I'll make you come to me sometimes now."

"You call, I'm here."

At the sound of a knock, we both looked up. Chase stepped into the room and closed the door behind him. He was subtle about twisting the lock, but I'd seen it done enough times that I didn't miss it.

"You heading home yet?" he asked.

"Nah. I like it here so much, I thought I might move in."

"Can I have your theater system, then?" Chase asked.

"What?" I feigned hurt. "You're not going to come live here with me? In my perfect new office?"

"Say *yes* now. She's going to spend half her life here anyway," Luke teased.

Chase sighed and came around to my side of the desk. "I don't know. I bet you don't even get 4K on those monitors."

waiting for it

"I do." Perk of the job—high-end gaming rig. "But fine. You can go live in my big empty house, all alone, and I'll stay here, in my cozy office, with Luke."

"Whoa. I never said *yes*." Luke moved to stand next to Chase. "I have my own cozy office."

I pouted.

Luke tugged my bottom lip down. "Speaking of awkward segues… I've been thinking that I don't like going home to separate beds. Ever."

"I don't think there's room for all three of us in here, and Chase obviously thinks my screens are too small." I knew where Luke was heading, but I wanted one more jab of fun.

"Your globes are exactly the right size." Chase dropped his gaze to my chest. "But I'm sure we can find plenty of ways to entertain ourselves here."

"Fine. I'll spell it out. I was thinking someplace besides the office," Luke said. "As in, all three of us living together in the same place."

Yes was on the tip of my tongue. "Did you have a specific place in mind?"

"I figured we'd all want a say in that. Maybe new memories in your place. Or a new place that's ours. It doesn't matter, as long as I get to come home to the two of you at night."

I looked at Chase, who grinned and said, "I'm in."

"Me too." I was going to be high on giddiness by the end of the night. Did that count as intoxication? Now I was being silly, too.

"Except for one thing…" Chase looked away.

"What thing?" I didn't like his hesitation, but he was up to something.

He nodded across the room. "I was hoping to try out your new couch. See what kind of *bounce* it has."

Me too. "You can do that anyway."

"Yeah?"

"Sure," Luke said. "You stay here, sleep on the couch, and we'll go celebrate."

Chase turned and covered Luke's hands with his own. Pressing in, he crushed his mouth to Luke's.

I groaned along with them. They didn't kiss often, but it was becoming more regular. "I can leave both of you here, if you need some privacy."

Luke stood, never breaking the kiss, and used his body to nudge Chase back. They finally split apart.

"Don't you dare go anywhere." Luke's tone was playfully threatening.

I was up for that challenge. "Or what?"

"I'll spank you."

I stood, placed my palms on my desk, and stuck my ass out. "Big words, big man."

Luke's palm connected with my backside before I'd registered that he moved. The *smack* that echoed through the room mingled with my gasp. We shouldn't do this in here, but that didn't stop us at any point in the last few months.

He tugged at my hair, pulling my head back. "Stay," he growled in my ear.

I whimpered. There was no room for argument. Not that I would argue. "Yes, sir."

"Good girl." Chase leaned in and kissed me hard. He caught my bottom lip between his teeth when he pulled away.

This was fun. A little kinky, a bit risky, and a lot of the most amazing anything I ever could have hoped for.

Fourteen-year-old me never would have believed me, if I'd told her when she was drooling over Chase, that this was our future. Then again, twenty-three-year-old me never would have bought that I'd be spending nights in sexy-boss's bed. But it was all real. *Our* future. All three of us together. And nothing could be more perfect.

About Allyson Lindt

USA Today Bestselling Author Allyson Lindt is a full-time geek and a fuller-time author. She's found her own happily ever after, where she and her spouse call their furbabies their children. Coffee is her task-master and random tangents are her muse. When she's not writing, she's fangirling over the latest superhero movies. She likes her stories with sweet geekiness and heavy spice, and loves a sexy happily-ever-after. Because cubicle dwellers need love too. Learn more about Allyson's books, including signing up for her newsletter, by visiting http://www.allysonlindt.com.